MORDEC THE CONQUEROR

THE THRILLING ADVENTURES OF MORDEC THE VIKING

Mordec Raids England
Mordec's Quest
Mordec and the Hidden Hand
Mordec and the Lost Boys
Mordec the Conqueror

THE THRILLING ADVENTURES OF
MORDEC THE VIKING

BOOK 5

MORDEC THE CONQUEROR

JILLIAN BECKER

Typesetting and Cover Design by
FormattingExperts.com

Published by Gothenburg Books
ISBN 978-1-7327275-8-8

contents

Mordec the Conqueror

To my grandchildren:
Matthew & Aaron Slipper
Jessica & Elizabeth Dilworth
Sam & Charlotte Westrop

warning of war

'Bad news, I'm sorry to say.'

Father Donlock came into the counting-house of Reginald, Earl of Linkard, at the usual time for their daily talk carrying a scroll with a large seal on it.

Father Donlock always looked serious, even grim, with his hollow cheeks and heavy lines bracketing his downturned mouth, and today he looked more solemn and unpleased then ever, frowning as he was with consternation. Yet he was not an ill-tempered man by any means, nor even a pessimistic one. He loved books, had voluntarily taken charge of the Earl's exceptionally well-stocked library, and was very well read in several languages. He did not entirely lack a sense of humour, but he was not known to laugh often.

So when the Earl said, 'And a very good morning to you too, dear Father, and yes it is a lovely day!', the priest looked up in surprise at what he thought a most inappropriate response to his announcement.

The Earl relented. 'Bad news, you say? Come and sit down and tell me about it.'

'Very bad. Very grave,' the priest said. 'This is a letter from the Abbott Alonso de Llama informing me that the Papal Army of the Redeemed—which he himself helped to form, I happen to know—is coming in full force to England on a fleet of fifty ships, due to sail from French ports within the next thirty days, to—I quote—"make war on the occupying Vikings, drive them from the land, and spread the faith throughout all the islands of the west". So it is war, my lord.'

'But not on us,' the Earl said. 'You are right that the news is bad. It will be bad for England. But we ourselves are not threatened—are we?'

'My lord, you know how it is with the Vikings. They will defend themselves of course, and when they make war, they do not pause to consider who may be innocent bystanders. They slaughter mercilessly. Indiscriminately. We are a small piece of Christendom. Do you think they will spare us?'

'We are on very good terms with our Viking neighbours—when they are here in occupation of their territory. We have a treaty with them, signed and sealed. They agreed never to bear arms into my earldom. And they have honoured the treaty for years now.'

'But will it not be different when they are under attack? Under threat of being dispossessed and expelled from the land? Yes, we know they can be peaceable friends. But we also know that they are terrifying enemies.'

'So you think that if they are attacked, they will attack us?'

'Us and every Christian, They will be intent on destroying us just as Abbott Alonso is intent on destroying them. And they are the more seasoned warriors. Trained from early youth to fight without mercy. To fight in so atrocious a manner that all who hear of it will fear to engage them.'

'And there is no stopping the Pope's army from coming here? Nothing we can say to prevent this invasion?'

'Abbott Alonso is a very determined man. He won't have any challenge to his authority. He's notoriously obstinate and—I dare to say it—reputed *with justification* to be as ruthless as the Vikings are.'

The Earl rose from the big oak chair where he sat at his worktable, went to the window, and gazed out at the peaceful green fields and scattered woods of his earldom. He clasped his hands behind him and was silent for a long while. Father Donlock said nothing. It was indeed, he approved, a time for the ruler to concentrate without interruption.

When the Earl returned to his chair, he seated himself slowly, spread his arms over the papers and scrolls awaiting his attention on the table, held his hands palm-up to show their emptiness, and sighed.

'Then we must prepare to defend ourselves,' he said. 'I can only hope that the authorities of the Church will not demand that our men join the Papal forces. Do you think you can extract a promise to that effect from the Abbott—or the Pope himself?'

'I will try, my lord. I will certainly try.'

The priest rose to go, but was stopped by the Earl with a question. 'Any other news? I was aware that couriers arrived before dawn. I expected to hear how the world marches. Though I had not expected it to march on us.'

Father Donlock drew another scroll from the sleeve of his cassock, unrolled it and glanced over it.

'There is still the immense reward of ten gold pieces offered—by the bellicose Abbott—for the delivery to him of Bjarwulf the Pirate. Oh, and one gold piece for another Viking. You will remember him—the boy who was nearly executed for entering the Earldom with weapons, some two or three years ago?'

'Mordec the Viking?' the Earl said. 'Jessica became quite fond of him. I thought he was a good lad. I was glad that his innocence was finally proved. What is he supposed to have done to be wanted by the Abbott?'

'It seems he murdered one of the Abbott's Black Monks. I find that hard to believe. He was not a murdering sort. He could read and write. He liked books. He even had some knowledge of other languages. But of course, as I was saying, the Vikings are raised to be fighters. He probably killed the monk in a duel of some kind. Apparently the Abbott sent a troop of his monks in pursuit of Mordec to a Viking stronghold in England, called …' the priest peered more closely at the parchment, 'the Castle of Yggdrasil, where they had been informed he was being given shelter. And the monks were ambushed and slaughtered to the last man. Yggdrasil, my lord,' the scholar priest could not help adding, 'is the name of the Tree of Life in Viking legend.'

'So this invasion is in revenge for the massacre of the monks?'

'It may be, in part, my lord. Although revenge is explicitly forbidden by our faith.'

'So he is acting immorally. Could we not appeal to the Pope on those grounds for His Holiness's intervention on our behalf?'

'My lord, the present Pope is a weak old man, a stuttering uncle of Abbot Alonso, who ordered the cardinals to elect him after the boy Pope was assassinated. Almost all the cardinals fear Abbot Alonso because he has his own regiment of Black Monks—and because he is ruthless. It is whispered in Rome that Abbot Alonso was behind the assassination. I'll go now and write the letter to the Abbot asking him not to conscript our men. I will ask him, but—I must be frank with you, my lord—I don't expect to win the concession. Now I must hurry to write my letter before the couriers start back to London.'

He bowed to the Earl and left the room. When he had quietly shut the door behind him, he stuffed the scrolls into his sleeve and stood for a few moments in the dim passageway with his eyes shut and his hands together in prayer. But prayer did not lighten his heart. Though he reproached himself for weakness of faith, he could not get rid of a sad doubt that prayer would keep the Earldom of Linkard, or any part of England, safe from the coming war.

the warning
comes to goosegarth

Sir Baz, the White Knight and self-appointed Champion of Queen Bertha of the East Fenreach (commonly known just as 'the Fenreach' as it had no counterpart to the west of it), was drilling the farmhands and a few 'idle, clumsy, useless village boys', as he called them—lads and grown men from the scattered villages of the Fenreach—in the art of combat, having lined them up in four rows of ten and one of three, in the farmyard of Goosegarth, the royal seat. He did this every now and then because Queen Bertha's granddaughter, Queen Lily, knew for sure they would need to fight the Vikings soon. He was a handsome man with very black skin and very red lips. He was not encased in his white armour, nor mounted on his white steed, but stood in sandals on the mucky ground between the henhouse and the pigpens clad only in a loose white tunic, facing his troops with a sword in his right hand and a freshly made hazel-bark whistle in the other.

'Again!' he commanded, and blew a tweet on his whistle.

The first row of troops raised their weapons—an assortment of pitchforks, scythes, fence-poles, leafy oak branches, horsewhips and one spindle—more or less in unison, and on a second tweet, brought them down, as hard as their instructor sliced the air with his flashing sword, as if upon the heads of enemies, and on a third tweet, they shouldered them and ran, some right, some left, to the back of the platoon.

'Well done Pompy and Colom!,' Sir Baz shouted. 'Two kills. The rest of you—your enemies are not even lying on the ground. Just three of them are rubbing their heads and all of them are laughing. Now they're coming at us with their teeth bared and a terrible glowering in their wicked eyes. Next row, advance'.

At the signal of the hazel-twig, the next ten strode forward. At a signal they stopped. At another, they raised their weapons. And Sir Baz had the whistle at his lips for one more little blow to command ten heavy blows, but he blew it not. He raised his left arm to shield his eyes form the sun as he looked along the track leading down to the yard from the stone fastness of Goosegarth farmstead. And yes, it was as he'd thought. Queen Bertha was coming, sitting sideways on her lioness, leaning over so that her head rested between the beast's ears. The big cat walked slowly, pad after pad, enjoying the stroll. The Queen's gown was of silk, the reds and golds of honey, flowing with light. Her black and silver hair was held at her nape—invisibly as yet to the adoring eyes of Sir Baz—with an amber clasp studded with carnelians. And on her feet she wore a sturdy pair of old stained leather boots made for work among the livestock in their lush mess.

Sir Baz held his sword upright in front of his face, the blade just touching the tip of his nose, then he swept it down to his side, and bowed to the lady.

Gracefully she dismounted, and the lioness, relieved of her light burden, padded off towards a thicket of thorn from within which grunts and cries were emerging, then stood stock still with her head lifted and her nostrils flared, sniffing to help her interpret the sounds.

'Good-day to you, Sir Baz!' Queen Bertha said, raising a hand also to salute the defence force. The men tipped their hats or pulled a forelock in return. The boys just stood and gaped. She turned back to Sir Baz. 'I have brought news.'

'News, my lady?'

She mounted the three steps of the henhouse, and turned on the top step to face them all.

'I bring news of war,' she called. 'Word has come by messenger from the Earl of Linkard that an army of the Church is coming from France to England to drive the Vikings out and seize their land, and to baptize all who have not yet been saved. The Vikings will resist. Those who have land in these parts will come to protect them. Neither the Church nor the Vikings will scruple to fight anywhere in the Fenreach. We will have to defend ourselves.'

Sir Baz dropped to one knee, not caring that the knee fell in a wet cowpat.

'I live only to defend you, my lady,' he proclaimed. He rose and swung an arm toward his platoon. 'And these men too are ready to die for you. Right, men?'

'Mmm' some of them mumbled. Learning to fight was one thing, fighting to the death quite another. They all looked uneasy.

'The answer's yes,' Sir Baz growled at them. 'Or I'll slice you into bacon.'

'Yes!' came an unwilling chorus that even the boys joined in.

'This will not come as a surprise to Lily,' Queen Bertha said. 'She's been expecting it for years. Where is she?'

Lily was in the midst of the thorn thicket, practising her swordplay on the bushes, which fought back viciously, so that her arms and legs, and even her face, were wounded by fine scratches. She emerged from the thicket, revealing that she was the source of the grunts and cries that had so bewildered the lioness, who now lay down in the warm dirt, her curiosity satisfied and her readiness to attack abandoned.

'Gran? What is it?' Lily called.

'War,' her grandmother called back.

'The Vikings are attacking us? At last!' Lily ran to Bertha full of excitement and joy.

'Not yet the Vikings,' Bertha said. 'The Church. The Pope has formed an army and is sending it to seize the Viking lands, and make Christians of us all.'

Lily stopped still and gazed up at Bertha, with a puzzled face.

'The Church? The Pope? Seize the Viking lands? And the Vikings aren't going to stop them?'

'I'm sure the Vikings will come to stop them. And they won't be all the Vikings put a stop to. The Fenreach will be their battlefield.'

'When ...?'

'Any day now. The Christians are on their way in fifty ships, it is said. By the time they get here, the Vikings will be waiting for them. That's my guess.'

Lily sprang up the steps of the henhouse, and embraced her grandmother with a shout of joy. The lioness interpreted the action as an attack on her mistress, so she rose and growled and got ready to spring on the attacker. But Queen Bertha stretched out her hand towards her, and the beast subsided.

'Will we or will we not die for our land and our Queen?' Sir Baz shouted to his men, who were no longer in orderly rows but gathering in clumps, asking each other worried questions. They fell silent. But then, 'Three cheers for our Queens,' Pompy cried out.

'Yes, three cheers for our Queens!' echoed Colom.

And three cheers rang out through the farmyard, startling the geese into a frightful barking, and the lioness into a mild convivial roar.

Lily smiled, waved, then turned to Bertha, took a deep breath, and said quietly, her eyes shining with excitement, 'Gus will be one of the commanders.'

Sir Baz had come close to the henhouse and heard what she said.

'And Mordec, Queen Lily?' he asked. 'What about Mordec? Won't he be a commander?'

Lily quickly shook her head. 'No, I don't think so. Mordec can read and write. He can understand maps.

I've seen him do it when we were on the island with Sam of the West. He'll stay with the older men to help them plan their battles. Anyway, I don't want him to come to any harm.'

'Many will come.' Bertha said gravely, but in a firm tone of voice, for she would not shrink from facing the threat. 'It will be a vast army. I have seen them, the Vikings, battle-hot, feverish with bloodlust, fearless killers. In war they are not men but ravening beasts. If the Pope thinks his army will easily defeat them, he has not been well informed. Even Vikings who are in love, who pour gold and precious gems into the laps of the ladies they woo, forget themselves, forget their love, forget all that has passed between them and those dearest to them, when the battle fury is upon them, Come now Lily, come Sir Baz, we must plan what to do. I know I can count on the Earl to help us as best he can. But the Earl is putting his faith in a treaty he made after the last war with the Vikings. A treaty with his Viking neighbours who have always been peaceable enough. They will be different now. We must not let him expect too much from that.'

She put her hand on the head of the lioness and started back along the dusty road to the stone house—a solid structure, but no fortress.

Sir Baz told his troops they were done for the day but he'd be coming to talk to them later. 'I must prepare you to fight with real weapons in a real war,' he warned them sternly. But he sighed as he turned away. 'Bows and arrows' he said to himself, 'maybe.'

Lily and Sir Baz followed Queen Bertha in silence. Sir Baz, having fought many a battle, was in serious mood. Lily was already in her imagination defending England from Gus, picturing them both in full armour and wielding glittering new swords.

the vikings prepare for war

The Vikings knew the day, the very hour, when the fifty ships carrying the Army of the Redeemed were to start for England from the ports of France with the aim of seizing the lands subdued by the Vikings and bringing the whole country into the realm of the Roman Christian Church.

They knew the size of the army, the weapons they held and those they planned to construct, and even the tactics they had practised in their small platoons in fields and forests.

And they intended to be waiting on the eastern shore of England before a single Redeemed soldier had set foot on English soil.

They had been kept informed by Sam of the West, who dispatched word of every step taken by the Commander-in-Chief of the invading army, Abbot Alonso de Llama, his neighbour on a small island off the coast of France. Sam's messages flew on the legs of pigeons to Julius the Troll in the far North, and Julius sent them with horsemen to Hauk the Meadmaker and his son Mordec. From their mead hall, which had become a communication centre, riders and runners, carts and boats hastened to the chiefs, the towns, the markets, the mead halls, the armourers, the fishermen, who heard the messages and in their turn sent others on, until all the North was informed, armed, and eager to go to war.

Queen Lily of the Fenreach was right that Mordec son of Hauk could understand maps. He could draw them too. He peered through the glasses he wore to help his shortsighted eyes see clearly on thin parchments the outlines of England that Julius the Troll supplied, and on it he made small drawings that indicated where villages, farms, castles, woods, rivers, hills, towns, stood—and, very importantly, churches and missions.

A small part of England he knew because he had been there. For the rest—books stacked on the table where the maps were made, told him what he needed to know. They were records of travellers' tales, trader's directions to their salesmen, church chronicles compiled by Christian missionaries.

Because he could do this, being literate among many who were not, Mordec was respected. He was only just seventeen (a winter, a summer, another winter and a spring having passed since he had come home from his willing and unwilling adventures abroad), but he was looked up to by older men because he could advise them where best to camp, which high ground commanded the widest view, where an ambush might be laid on a hillside or in a wood.

But he would not be content to help the Viking army by working at a table. He had every intention of fighting. He had ordered swords and new armour—having long grown out of the first suit made for him when he first went to raid England, where, far from terrifying the English, he had been terrified himself by the threat of a dreadful death only narrowly escaped.

Now he would return there, not as a raider but as a conqueror. He was as determined as any man in the Viking army that they would win the war—perhaps even more than any other because the Commander-in-Chief of the Church army, Abbot Alonso, was his personal enemy.

While he had been on the island where both Sam of the West and the Abbot dwelt, he had saved his friend Gus son of Hakon from a murderous attack by killing one of the Abbot's Black Monks. The Abbot lusted for revenge, and had spread word of a reward of gold to anyone who would bring Mordec alive to him.

So Mordec drilled along with all the others. They practised combat every day, while they waited for their Commander-in-Chief, Tostig son of Tostig the Conqueror, to come with the main strength of the army. Their harbour had been chosen as the one from which the force would sail. More ships arrived every day at Trygghaven, far too many to come close to land, so most anchored out at sea.

Every son of the North over the age of fourteen had to join the army except a very few who were totally blind or had lost the use of arms or legs. (Even so, some who had the use of only one arm, and two who had only one leg, declared they were going to fight, because it was what every man was born to do, go to war; and if he was killed by the enemy, he was sure to go to Valhalla, feast with Odin himself, and live there for the rest of time among the heroes.) The women would stay home to care for the children and guard the property of the warriors.

And—oh, yes!—there was another exception among the men: a tall strong youth, seventeen years old, who could see perfectly, and move swiftly, and wield weapons with extraordinary skill—and what was even more had valuable experience of fighting real enemies at risk of losing his life. And this man was to stay behind with the blind, the lame, the women and children! Why? Because the law forbade him to join the army.

That man was Gus son of Hakon—the friend whose life had been saved by Mordec, and the natural commander whom Queen Lily was dreaming of meeting on the battlefield.

How could this be? A man who would be so great an asset to the army; a man who longed to fight and could fight so well—forbidden to go to the war? It sounded so strange to all newcomers who saw him standing aside, watching the others training for battle.

Those who asked why were told the reason for it.

The tall young man with yellow hair was being punished for committing a grave crime.

What had he done to deserve so shameful a punishment?

The answer came: he had attempted to murder another Viking; his victim had survived the attempt, and having the right to decide the punishment, had decreed that he was not to join the army. 'Ah!' the enquirers said, no longer feeling the young man was being unjustly treated, though they might still pity him—which he guessed they did, to his further shame.

It was indeed a cruel and humiliating punishment for Gus, who aspired to be a great warrior as other men did to be rich and powerful. But he made no complaint. He said not a word against the man who had ordered his harsh punishment, because that man was Mordec, who had saved his life.

Some of those who had been his friends since childhood asked Gus what no grown up or even his own father and mother would ask him: *why* he had committed the crime. Why had he locked Mordec in the hold of a burning ship and left him to die? But Gus did not answer the question. He only said, 'I did it. It was wrong. I have no complaint about my punishment.'

Mordec and Gus avoided each other. If they found themselves somewhere at the same time, they did not exchange a word or even a look.

Gus spent long hours in the sheds of the armourers, of which there were suddenly three near the harbour. He would watch men choose weapons, order and try on armour. And now and then he would advise a young lad who had never wielded a sword in anger where to aim, how to strike. And all the while his face was set hard. All who knew him thought that he was bravely refusing to show

how deep was his regret that he could not join the rest and sail with them to war.

There was, however, one who believed he knew what had moved Gus to commit his crime: Hengist son of Hengist the Fisherman, one of two who had travelled with Mordec and Gus through France and Italy on a quest to find Queen Lily's mother, and had chosen to stay there with the Lombards under the patronage and protection of Mordec's grandfather, Adam.

He had arrived back in Trygghaven very soon after the news of the Church's planned invasion of England had reached him—early though that was, and far though he had had to travel. How had he heard of the plan, he was asked. To which he would only reply that news from all the world poured into the Lombard town night and day. Travellers came to Adam's counting-house, messengers flew in and out.

Hengist had an explanation for what Gus had done to Mordec.

'It was sheer jealousy,' he confided to ten or twelve curious enquirers. 'Gus was driven mad with jealousy. That's all. I mean, anyone could see that Gus was in love with Lily. He thought Mordec had made her care more for him.'

'Did she?' some asked.

'I don't know, but Mordec and Lily were always laughing together. It drove Gus crazy to think they were laughing at *him*. Horsa and I—we told him it wasn't true. But, well—we didn't know what happened after they left us. But when we heard all about it, we knew why he'd done it. We could almost have seen it coming.'

Nobody asked Gus if what Hengist said was true.

Hengist worked in one of the armouries. He had new ideas for both arms and armour, but the older men did not want anything 'new-fangled', just the tried and trusted sort of thing they and their fathers before them had always used.

One evening, when almost everyone went home to dinner and only Hengist was left in the armoury, working on something of his own design, for his own pleasure as he liked to do when the hours he was paid to work were over, Gus came in and sat down near him. For a while neither of them spoke.

It was Hengist who broke the silence, saying while his hands went on with their task:

'I'm going to change my name.'

'You've already changed it once,' Gus reminded him.

'Not exactly changed it. I asked you to stop calling me Little Hengist since Big Hengist was not with us. Now I'm home again, Big Hengist is here and I want an entirely different name.'

'What name? Have you thought of one?'

'Daedalus. It's a Greek name. Daedalus was the father of Icarus who made wings for himself and his son, out of feathers and wax. Icarus flew too close to the sun and the wax melted and he fell into the sea and drowned. My master Adam the Lombard, Mordec's grandfather, told me the story. Daedalus was a great inventor and craftsman. A "fabricator", Adam called him. So I am Daedalus the Fabricator.'

'Tell the Skald, and he'll spread it round.'

'I did.'

Silence fell again for a while as Daedalus the Fabricator worked on.

Then Gus spoke:

'Where is Horsa?'

'Who're you asking?'

'You. There's no one else here but you and me.'

'Call me by my name and then I'll answer you.'

'Oh, of course. Daedalus, great Fabricator! Pray tell me, where is Horsa son of Harvald who stayed with you at the house of Adam the Lombard in Gaudium Brevis in Italy?'

'You mocking me?'

'No.'

'Just Daedalus will do.'

'So where is he? *Daedalus*?'

'I don't know. That's the truth. Nobody knows, not even Adam. The day after Adam told us that the Army of the Redeemed was marching to the French ports to sail to England and expel the Vikings from their lands, Horsa disappeared. He took all his things. All his weapons. He must have got a cart to fetch him before we woke that morning. He left a note for Adam but not for me. He left nothing for me. We hadn't quarrelled or anything. He just didn't want me to know where he was going.'

'What did the note to Adam say? Do you know?'

'I read it so many times I know every word. It said, "I have to go away. I am forever in your debt, illustrious lord Adam. I have tried to serve you well in return for taking me into your house and bringing great warriors to me who have taught me all I need to know. Farewell. I will return one day." I thought that he must have set out for home, to join the army. He could be a captain, a general even. I told Adam I must also go and fight with the Viking army. I said I would have gone with Horsa, but Adam said he didn't think I'd find Horsa here. He said if that was his plan he would have taken me with him. And Adam was right of course. He's not here.'

'What did he mean when he said "I tried to serve you well in return"? What did he do for Adam?'

'When the Army of the Redeemed came last year against the Lombards, a whole regiment of Vikings turned up to defend us from Nebula under the command of one Captain Rorick, who had been one of Eyiolf's officers. We were expecting the enemy to come against us. The Church hates the Lombards. But these Vikings were ready for them, and some of my devices were standing loaded with rocks and wasps on the walls of Brevis. The Army of the Redeemed must have sent scouts who saw how well we were defended. So they left us alone, bypassed us, went on to the next town which was full of Moors. Rorick's Vikings followed them, and Horsa went with them, and they met the Christians on the streets of the town, and fought them and defeated them. They say there weren't many live Christians left. Horsa came back without a scratch on him and claimed to have killed six Christians. He told Adam that he would always protect him and the Lombards. He claimed that any enemy who just heard that Horsa the Christian Slayer was armed and ready for him, would run away. He thought of himself as Adam's guard, though he hadn't actually had to save Adam himself. He's a big boaster, Horsa son of Harvald.'

'He's a man we—I mean our army could use. Perhaps he'll turn up yet. Perhaps he's gone ahead of us to England and is waiting there in hiding.'

Daedalus shrugged. 'Who knows?'

'What are you doing?'

'You can see what I'm doing. I'm painting on leather armour.'

'With such dull colours. Sort of dust and lichen. That won't frighten the enemy.'

'The idea is not to frighten him but to be invisible to him. These colours match the fields and woods. A man who creeps about in this will not easily be seen from a distance.'

'Is it for yourself or has someone ordered it?'

'Oh, I won't use it—I'll work away from the battlefield. No one's ordered this. That's why I'm making it in my spare time. I hope someone will have the sense to try it out.'

Gus rose. 'I'm going home to dinner now. G'night—*Daedalus*.'

Daedalus gave no answer. He went on painting the armour the colours of 'dust and lichen'.

the arrival of
harald goldmountain

It was Mordec who received—by messenger from Julius the Troll—the first news of the approach of the main body of the army under the command of Tostig son of Tostig, with instructions to make the chief's orders widely known by announcement in the mead hall, the shipyard, the harbour, and to the armourers. The priest and the Skald must proclaim them wherever they went. The captains of the ships must be personally informed.

The orders were that officers and important persons must be billeted in the best houses, but the men would pitch tents on the cliffs and heathlands. Tostig himself would reside in the biggest house with Olaf the Shipbuilder, and the main paymaster of the whole expedition, Harald Goldmountain, would reside in the next best homestead with Hauk the Meadmaker.

These arrangements would continue until all the fleets were fully equipped and supplied, and the whole army ready to sail. That would have to be in no more than fourteen days from the date of the Commander's arrival, because the army must be in England before the enemy left the ports of France.

The messenger reached the Meadmaker's gate at dinner time. Mordec took the scroll to the table and read it aloud to his father and mother and the two boys, his little brother Eyrin and the lost boy Leif who had quickly become as one of the family. Hauk and Estrid received the news first with frowns of worry, then, looking at each other, with shrugs. They had no choice but to expect the houseguest and make ready for him.

Leif was excited by the news, clapped his hands, laughed aloud. He felt caught up in a great drama in the Viking world to which he so happily now belonged. Only little Eyrin went on steadily eating, thinking his own thoughts.

Estrid told how she had met the great man in her youth in Italy, when he had come to consult with her father Adam the Lombard, and make use of his services as a protector of money and treasure. She had heard from her father, in a letter brought to her (along with a lavish gift of gold and jewels) by Hengist son of Hengist, that the armies of both the Church and the Vikings were already on the move. But she had not heard until now that Harald Goldmountain was with the Viking force.

'He was a handsome man, Harald Goldmountain,' Estrid said. 'Rich even in those days, young as he was, because his father was quite a rich man himself and gave Harald the money to start his many ventures. Harald wasn't stuck up and aloof as you might expect such a man to be. And he wasn't tight-fisted. I remember he liked to throw small coins in a shower over children playing in the streets. And I remember his laugh, loud and funny in itself, so everyone used to laugh when he did.'

'He will be good company then,' Hauk said.

'If he hasn't changed,' said Estrid.

'We must *go*, Mordec. We must go and tell everyone what the message says,' Leif urged, bolting his food. 'It's urgent.'

'Not so urgent it can't wait a few minutes. I'll go after dinner.'

'Don't eat so slowly then!'

'Sorry, my owner,' Mordec said, and went on eating at his usual rate.

'I'm coming with you, aren't I?'

'Hmmm. Well, since you've given me permission to go, I'll give you permission to come with me,' Mordec conceded.

He memorized the orders before he and Leif set out for the shipyard, where Olaf and his men were still at work. They went on from house to house repeating the orders again and again, Leif joining in the recitation when he too had them by heart. But soon they found they could stop, because the news had travelled ahead of them, and people were coming out of their houses and milling about, telling each other all they knew, asking questions no one could answer, and making up answers out of their dreads and wishes.

Hauk took the scroll to the mead hall, stuck it on the wall with a dagger, and late in the evening when the hall was full, read it aloud for the benefit of those (the most) who could not read it themselves and might not yet have heard the urgent instructions, of which there were very few by then.

The name of Harald Goldmountain caused the most stir. He was reputed to be the richest man in the North, perhaps in the world; richer, some said, than the Caliph of the Moors, than the Pope in Rome. He owned fleets of ships, vast stretches of land, harbours, mines, farms—*and*, the wags would say, the Caliph and the Pope.

The tax collectors' wages were paid by him, and the taxes were brought to him before they were handed on to the kings and chiefs to be spent on their own upkeep and the common good, for which intermediary service Harald Goldmountain kept back a well-deserved and substantial fee.

Twenty slaves or servants, ten men and ten women, arrived some hours before their master, and pitched tents in the meadow nearest the house.

Hauk's horses and ponies withdrew into the shade of an oak grove in one corner of the field and gazed mournfully at the tents that covered so much of the grass.

Then came pack-mules laden with furs and food, barrels and weapons, for which Hauk had difficulty finding storage places. The mules were led away again by the swarthy slaves who had walked them all the way from the city of Hedeby.

Then a dark-skinned overseer with a bald head, who walked with a heavy limp in his ballooning trousers, and wore large gold rings hanging from his long earlobes and a jewelled scimitar stuck through a wide purple sash, was suddenly there, and everywhere, supervising the distribution of the goods and giving orders to the serving men and women. He was promptly obeyed. Cripple though he was, he moved with agility and speed, and nothing, it seemed, escaped his notice.

Unasked, he gave his name to Hauk. 'I am Bernie, illustrious lord,' he said in a rich, deep voice, and with a quick nod of his bald head in lieu of a bow.

He entered the house and at once started rearranging almost everything in it. Hauk made no protest. He understood. Harald Goldmountain would not be sharing his home but taking it over. So Hauk and Mordec moved some furniture and personal things into outhouses, and made up beds of fur over fresh straw at one end of the stable for Eyrin and Leif.

'I'll have to cook our meals outside,' Estrid said to Hauk as they watched a crate of herrings being carried into the house.

Bernie overheard her. 'You will not need to cook, illustrious lady,' he told her. 'We have brought our cooks. They will prepare everything, and the Master may want you to eat with him at your table.'

So they were to be guests in their own house.

To welcome the great man, Estrid dressed in a tunic of grey silk and a cloak of blue wool closed at the waist with an ornate jewelled brooch, and she braided lavender in her long hair. Hauk and Mordec wore their body-armour of iron mail over leather to show their readiness to go to war. Eyrin and Leif were tidily clothed in woollen tunics and leather shoes.

The day wore on, savoury smells filled the house, and still the Master did not appear. The twilight came down that would last through the hours of what was nevertheless called the night. A messenger brought the news that Commander-in-Chief Tostig had arrived at the house of Olaf the Shipbuilder where he had been greeted by a long line of grandees including the priest and the Skald. Thousands of soldiers were lighting fires in front of their tents on the headlands and heathlands.

By this time Eyrin, and even Leif for all his eagerness to miss nothing that was to happen that night, had grown heavy eyed. And both of them were hungry. A manservant dressed in the Goldmountain livery of purple and white brought them heaped plates of pickled herring and braised elk, after which Eyrin fell asleep on the grass. Hauk picked him up and carried him, and Estrid took Leif's hand and led him—protesting in a sleepy voice that he wasn't tired—to their beds.

It was past midnight when the sound of drums and trumpets reached the ears of all who were still awake—and woke the rest as it grew louder. Sleepy servants came out of tents, barefooted, yawning, rubbing their eyes.

Lanterns were brought out of the houses. Swinging lights and flaming torches were to be seen coming with a procession along the rough road leading to the gate, casting sweeping shadows, now large now small, on trees and walls and the people in the train.

Through the pale light of the early morning they advanced, dark grey grooms leading four pairs of dark grey horses pulling a high cart, higher than a house, on which there was a wide seat of bright gold lined with cushions of purple silk and pure white ermine—but nobody was seated on it. Grandly, ceremoniously, it was drawn, swaying this way and that, empty of a passenger.

Lines of dark grey trumpeters marched beside the cart, lines of dark grey drummers marched behind them, and between their lines, treading slowly but steadily to the beat of the music, were clumps of guardsmen in dark grey mail, followed by clumps of slaves or servants, and all of them covered in the dark grey road dust, the uniform of everything and everyone from the leading horses and their grooms to the last torch-bearer. Not only did the dust cover the feet and clothes and helmets and hats of the marchers but also, as thickly, their faces and hair and hands.

Only the beautiful golden bench with its purple and white cushions escaped the clouds stirred up by the hooves and marching feet. It soared above them, lit by lanterns held over it on tall rods by men on both sides of it wading through the dust. He—the Master—should have been up there, illuminated in his finery: Harald Goldmountain of almost legendary fame. Surely he was there! He had merely become invisible. He would suddenly appear seated on the purple and white cushions.

But no. The horses stood still. The trumpets and the drums ended their music with one last long note, one last bang.

From the midst of the slaves and servants emerged a dark grey dusty figure, big and heavy, surely a man—but young or old, no one could tell. Was this a messenger who would tell them where the Master was? Why he had been delayed? Or that there had been an accident?

The grey messenger, a big man, strongly built, strode in through the open gateway and stopped in front of Estrid, not Hauk. He knelt on one knee in the grass, took her right hand and carried it to his dusty lips; then rose, flung off his hat and cloak of dust, brushed most of it from his face, and laughed.

It was an immense laugh, a laugh that bred more laughs which broke out all around him, and more still in the house and among the trees and it was heard all the way to the meadow, and down the line of the halted procession on the road.

It was a laugh that started with a guffaw, hiccupped into a chortle which was followed by a series of hoots and ended in another chortle.

Estrid laughed. Mordec laughed. And Hauk couldn't help smiling though he watched the antics of the dusty man with bewilderment, and his smile changed to a frown when the stranger dropped Estrid's hand, stepped right up to her, put his dusty arms round her waist and lifted her like a child while he again laughed his enormous raucous laugh.

'Little Esther, don't you remember me, Harald, who used to make you laugh?'

'I do, I do.' Esther said, catching her breath as he gently put her down. 'Who could forget *you*, Harald Goldmountain?'

Now he came to Hauk with his arms held wide. 'And you are Hauk, her husband?' His arms went round Hauk's neck and drew him to a dusty chest.

Then, clasping Hauk's shoulders, he said loudly, 'I've heard of you from Adam the Lombard, so good and sober a father, and good guardian of gold, who would not approve of the cost of such a prank as this.'

He gave the shoulders in his hands a friendly shake. 'I've surprised you, yes? But you are not angry? No, we will be close friends you and I.'

He let go of Hauk and turned to Mordec. 'And who is this with eyeglasses and a soft young beard?' Keeping a few feet away, he said quietly, 'You must be Mordec the Hero, of whom the Skalds sing.' And without waiting for an answer, he bowed.

Mordec wondered if he was being mocked, but Harald's suddenly serious face did not suggest it. 'I—yes—illustrious lord, I'm Mordec son of Hauk,' he said, and in the manner he had learnt in a royal court, he returned the bow.

Harald straightened up, and as suddenly as he had become ceremonious, he became simply friendly. With an arm across Mordec's back he moved towards the house. 'Come,' he said, 'we need to wet our throats and I must wash off this *road* I am wearing.' Again he laughed his loud laugh, again making all who heard it join in.

His other arm gathered Hauk to his side. Walking them into their own house, he shouted for 'Water, then meat and wine!' And soon he was seated, dressed in fresh clothes, his yellow hair—which sat on his head like a helmet, sweeping low over his forehead and covering the nape of his neck—shining under the lantern light. He held a drinking horn high as he toasted his host, his hostess, the Viking army, and 'all the pretty maidens who will fall in love with Mordec'.

This last pledge he followed with the great guffaw and its sequence, which set everyone else laughing yet again. He looked round happily at all the laughing faces.

'You will tell me your stories, Hauk, Mordec, my friends, while we eat and drink.'

And so they did, and only got to their beds when the day grew bright.

mordec rides with harald

The dark grey horses that had pulled Harald Goldmountain's empty chair turned out when dusted and groomed to be handsome, high-stepping, pale brown stallions with white tails and manes. Harald ordered his grooms to have them ready for riding after an early breakfast of herrings on black bread and a deep horn of ale brought to him in bed by Bernie.

The saddles were dyed purple, and the cloths beneath them were purple trimmed with gold. Harald sent for Mordec and invited him, in a tone more suited to a command than a request, to ride with him on a matching steed.

Mordec (watched over by Leif) was spending most of his days on the cliffs with the other young men of Trygghaven practising the arts of war, so the request that was like a command had to be brought to the instructor for his permission for Mordec to take a day off. As it came from Harald Goldmountain, the permission was granted immediately, and the handsome stallions set off with Harald and Mordec in the purple saddles.

Behind them rode ten men, grooms and armed guards on mounts of various sorts and sizes, and when news of the excursion spread, which it rapidly did, a little crowd of boys followed at a short distance, some walking and some riding. Leif, who never let Mordec out of his sight for long if he could help it, sat happily on his shaggy grey and white pony that he had named Snorri the Second, Eyrin's pony being Snorri the First.

Harald had a particular destination in mind. He moved steadily southward, keeping his horse at a walking pace so he could talk to Mordec as they rode side by side.

The night before, Mordec had told him how he had journeyed, with three Viking companions and a young English queen, over land and sea to Italy; had fought a battle; evaded capture; rested awhile with Adam the Lombard; paraded down Italy in the long retinue of the boy Pope; and had failed in his quest to get the young queen's mother back to England.

As the night brightened into full day, the great man had become too sleepy and too full of wine and mead to understand everything that was said to him, but he now recalled being told by someone that Mordec had forbidden a young strong Viking, who had been with him on the unsuccessful quest, to join the army.

He asked Mordec about this now, and Mordec told him, in as few words as would do, the sorry tale of what had happened on the island where Sam of the West lived alongside Abbot Alonso de Llama; how to save his friend Gus's life, he had killed an assailant; and how, after that, Gus had left him locked up to die on the burning ship called The Good Ship Good. He ended abruptly by saying that ('as you see') he had managed to free himself from confinement and had reached dry land safely.

'And your father went to hunt for you over all the western seas? I have not yet heard the Skald's saga about you, but your mother told me that. So of course it is true.'

'Yes.'

'And he found you?'

'He found where I had been, and learnt that I was on my way home, and he came back and found me here.'

'And this Gus son of Hakon …?'

'He confessed. He was found guilty by the Thing. It was for me to decide his punishment.'

'And you decided that he may not fight with us?'

'Gus is a warrior born,' Mordec said. 'He wants nothing more than to go to England and fight. He longs to command men in battle.'

'So it might be said that you condemned him to the worst of all punishments for him?'

'Yes.'

Harald expected Mordec to explain, to make some excuse for his severity perhaps. When it became plain that Mordec intended to say no more, Harald turned his head to look at his companion. But Mordec had his gaze fixed straight ahead through his glasses, and his face remained expressionless.

They rode in silence for some distance, and came to a dry river. Their horses scrabbled down the bank, stamped over the cracked earth on the river bed and leapt up the other side.

There Harald paused to let his guards and grooms catch up. They could hear the rabble of boys approaching, but did not wait for them. As soon as everyone in his escort was with him, Harald rode on.

Feeling that there was now a stiffness besilver tween him and Mordec, Harald said, 'I know now why they sing about you, young Mordec. You are made of stern stuff and are perhaps wise beyond your years. I wouldn't care to cross you—though of course in any contest between me and you, I'd win, because I am older and richer than you. Experience and money are both powerful, and together they are almost unbeatable.'

Mordec smiled. 'I cannot think of any reason why you and I should be in contest with each other,' he said. 'I can look to your experience and wealth to help the Viking cause—which is my cause and your cause—and you will perhaps find a use for my talents.'

'Which are?'

'Stern stuff and wisdom beyond my years?' Mordec suggested.

Upon which the great man threw back his head and laughed his enormous laugh. As usual it made everyone laugh. The boys heard it from afar and hurried to catch up and know what the joke was. But Harald moved on.

'All this land,' he said, sweeping an arm from east to west, 'as far as you can see in all directions from this side of the old river, is mine. It is like a great island, with sea on two side of it and rivers on two sides. Though the one river has run dry because of a landfall in the mountain range out of sight in the east. We started farms here, moving Lapps from the far north who wanted to live a settled life into home-steads that I had built for them. Viking craftsmen came to sell their services and artifacts, and a village grew up.'

He pointed to some ruins.

'Look over there, can you see those tumbled stones? They were once part of that village. There—broken walls. And over there the skeletons of houses with-out roofs. You can see the black where fire scorched them.'

He rode no nearer, sat still, loosened his reins to let his horse graze.

There was a sadness in his voice which told Mordec he was intent on his own thoughts, and should not be interrupted with questions.

'We came to live here for a time,' he went on, 'more than two years as it worked out. I and my wife Gudrun. I married late in life. She was young. Our child was born here. We named the place Haraldsholm. I thought we'd live here always. We hoped for more children, and I planned to build a big house. I had to be away often because I had other farms to visit, and my first silver mine. But I thought of this as home. When my little boy was two years old, I had a small ship built for him.'

'A small ship?' Mordec repeated sharply.

'Yes. Olaf the Shipbuilder was an apprentice lad then. I forget now where he put up the shed he worked in. It was some distance from the village. He was only a prentice, and he said the little ship would be his masterpiece. He did a good job. It was almost finished when last I saw it. I wonder if it's still there. Of course it was too early for my little boy to sail in it, but I wanted to give him everything. I bought ponies for him—and a small sword that Gudrun hid away somewhere, and …'

Mordec could keep his curiosity in check no longer. 'What happened?'

Harald was silent for so long, Mordec thought he either hadn't heard the question or didn't want to answer it.

'Raiders,' Harald said at last. 'The country was invaded by a gang of foreign raiders. They came from the south. They were of no particular tribe or country or creed. They came from far and near and were united only in villainy. They had no purpose other than plunder. We Vikings did not expect such gangs would dare to come to our country and attack us. We had a vain conviction that our reputation as fierce and ruthless warriors—and raiders ourselves—would keep us safe. We set no guards. We had our swords but no armour. How foolish we were! I was away when they came in the dark of winter, by sea, and then on foot to the village. They robbed the houses, razed the village and drove off the cattle and horses. Two of our men survived and fled, and brought news to me of the raid. They had left before the slaughter and the burning, and could not say if the women had been killed or taken as slaves with the children.

I came to see what was left of my home and seek some trace of Gudrun. What I found was one wounded raider left behind.'

He paused, then looking straight ahead he said, 'You've met him.'

'Bernie?'

Harald nodded. 'I intended to kill him when I got everything he knew out of him. He told me that no women had been spared, only children under ten years old, and they had been taken to be sold. Were you one of the killers, I asked him. No, he said. He was clumsy with a sword so his job was to pack and load the loot, and fire the houses with the bodies in them when they were ready to flee. He said that in one house he found a woman alive and holding a sword. It was she who slashed his leg so he could neither run nor walk. His shouts brought armed men to the house and they attacked the woman, but she fought back and it took three of them to kill her. Was she a tall woman, with honey-coloured hair? I asked him. She was, he said. I was sure he was speaking of Gudrun.'

He paused for a few moments, then went on.

'His companions rode off without him, telling him he was useless to them since he could only crawl. He crawled from house to house, throwing straw inside them and setting it on fire. He saved one house for himself, with a little store of food. He expected he would soon die. He saw no reason not to tell me the truth. I think he even hoped that I would kill him rather than leave him to starve. But a strange whim came upon me. I would keep the man alive after all, simply because he was the last person to see Gudrun alive and witness her bravery. I took him. He healed well enough to work. He has been my slave ever since. A good slave. I became quite fond of him.'

He drew up the head of his horse.

'I'm growing hungry. We'll go back now.'

As he was turning Mordec asked him. 'Your child—how old would he be now?'

'He'd be about the same age as those young rascals over there. The one on the grey and white pony would be what—eight?'

'About that. What was your son's name?'

'I wanted to call him Harald, but my wife had other ideas. I sent hunters in all directions throughout the next spring and summer seeking the raiders and their captives. But the gang had broken up, the slaves were sold, and no doubt sold on and on. I gave up hope. Now let's test the speed of these horses from here to the dry river.'

* * *

Bernie loved his master. He strove to serve him perfectly. To this end, he had learnt to count, to write numbers and necessary words.

Little Eyrin was drawn to this strange person. He followed him. He went barefoot because Bernie did, and the two of them padded softly about the house and orchard. Eyrin even copied Bernie's limp sometimes behind his back—not in mockery but to experience how it felt. Bernie called him Nino, but wouldn't explain why. Sometimes he gave his small companion a honeyed mulberry 'to taste', or a strip of white bread crisped in the fat of sheep kidneys.

At first the child had wondered at the man's strangeness, his looking like nobody else he had seen in his short life; but he soon came to like his quiet friendliness; and above all he was entranced by his counting. Daily this strange man counted aloud the pots and pans; the knives and spoons; the carcasses of lambs and oxen, pigs, chickens and geese that were unloaded from carts and brought into the kitchen; the bundles of roots and leaves and herbs laid out for the cooks; the garments of his lord that went into the wash and came out of it. Eyrin counted with him: 'One, two, three, four …'

One day as Bernie was about to count the spoons, Eyrin had gone up to them before him and counted loudly: 'Two, four, six, eight … and finally shouted the total with triumph. 'It takes half the time that way, Bernie,' he said.

'Who taught you how to do that, Nino?'

'You did,' Eyrin said.

It was Bernie's turn to wonder.

Bernie would talk to him as if he were a grown-up.

'The salt is getting low. If we don't get some soon it will be a disaster. I've asked for it twice. The traders don't care about small orders like ours, they have the huge orders for the soldiers on the cliffs. They forget that my master pays for all of it.'

'But your orders are really big,' Eyrin said, trotting after him and meaning to console him. 'You get a whole ox every day. We get only one for the long winter and cut it up and rub salt into the parts and smoke them in the chimney. And one pig. We get a pig too. And some fish. An ox and a pig and some fish that we cut up and rub with salt and smoke in the chimney have to last us the whole long winter.'

'And very good it tastes, doesn't it, Nino my dear?'

'It does, Bernie. I wish we had some now so I could give it to you.'

It was true what Bernie said about the traders and their big orders. Merchants, carriers and farmers far and near were prospering as never before in living memory. Hengist the Fisherman bought new boats and took on more crews consisting of prentices, bondsmen and slaves.

Bernie made sure that Estrid, though she was no longer welcome in her own kitchen, got a lavish share of whatever was cooked and brewed in it to feed her family.

Late in the evening of the day Mordec had gone riding with Harald, as he sat with Hauk and Estrid on the grass under an apple tree enjoying the soft light and sipping a nightcap of their own mead, Mordec related what Harald had told him. Leif and Eyrin were asleep in their beds.

'Did he say what his wife had named their son?' Estrid asked.

'No.'

Hauk said, 'There must be hundreds of eight-year-old orphan boys who would dearly like to be the son of Harald Goldmountain. For all we know they present themselves to him every few days.'

'So we mustn't even think about it?' Estrid asked.

'Not even think about it.' Hauk said. You agree do you? Both of you?'

Estrid and Mordec nodded.

'Pity though that the little ship that I found, my Foal of the Foam, is not mine after all,' Mordec said softly. 'It belongs to Harald's son, wherever he is. Maybe it belongs to my owner, Leif.'

'Sh!', said Estrid, putting a finger to her lips.

the first battle

Sam Gaudin was famously known as the great magician Sam of the West—or the Red Magician because he had dark red hair. He was not in fact a magician—indeed he did not believe in magic at all—but was truly a scientist.

Scientists were rare, and whatever they accomplished by applying the laws of nature was put down by public opinion to magic.

Sam accepted this on the common sense grounds that he could not, as far as he could see at present, do anything about it; and in any case it did not matter what people thought of him as long as they did not accuse him of using his powers to do evil. For that, the Church of Rome inflicted terrible punishments.

The eyes and ears of the Church were everywhere. Abbot Alonso de Llama, Sam's neighbour on the island where they both lived in a towering edifice of stone, had accused him of being in league with the Devil to acquire forbidden knowledge. But try as he might, the Abbot could produce no proof that would convince the present Pope, an old man who sat sleepily on the Chair of St. Peter. Although it was Abbot Alonso who caused the old man to dream of bringing all England under his sway, he resisted giving the Abbot too much authority in matters of heresy.

Not just England, but all of the Western Isles must, the Holy Father ordained, be brought into the loving embrace of the Catholic Church; but most of all he wanted the godless English—many of whom pretended to be Christians but did little more about it than accept baptism, marriage, and burial from their priests, and 'forget' to pay their tithes—to fall at the feet of Christ.

Now he was about to send an army to England to suppress all opposition, subdue rebellion, clear the way for the establishment of monasteries and the building of churches; and either force the conversion of the Vikings who occupied large portions of the land, or drive them altogether out of the country. After that, he would send missionaries to them in their own strongholds in the north.

The forming and training of the army had begun before his time. The very young Pope who had preceded him had allowed Abbot Alonso de Llama to start conscripting thousands of men, with the aid of kings, dukes and German barons in every part of central and southern Europe. Alonso gave it the name 'the Army of the Redeemed', and had sent his black habited monks hither and thither across the continent to preach the holy duty of bringing England under the discipline of the Cross.

The ships were ready, in ports all along the channel coast of France, to carry the soldiers over to England. The men were converging on them from every part of Christendom.

Of course they hoped that with luck they would not be attacked at sea; that the Vikings would not be ready enough, have gathered ships and men enough, to risk a sea battle with so large a fleet spread over so much of the channel. But they could not depend on it, and what with the movement of people bearing gossip, and the visible gathering of seacraft, it was unlikely that news of the intended invasion would not spread to the north.

Abbot Alonso himself expected that report of the preparations would have reached the most northern fjords of the Viking lands well before the date set for the sailing. He thought it possible that even that date might be known to them; for it had occurred to him at last that if he could listen through tubes inserted in the shared wall between his abbey and Sam's tower to catch something self-incriminating that Sam might say, so too could Sam listen to what was being said on his side of the same wall. And Sam had friends among the Vikings. So he had the listening-tubes blocked off, and his wall covered with sound-muffling tapestries.

Because of these precautions, he was confident that a top secret plan of his own to send an advance unit of a hundred men in three ships to establish a firm foothold on the English coast two days before the general sailing, was not known to Sam, or to anyone he didn't have to trust with his orders. His target was a particular castle against whose occupants he held a personal grudge. He did not even inform the Pope of his intention to have it taken by stealth at night.

And Sam would not have known of it, had not a message reached him written by an unknown hand. The informant must have been someone who came and went often from the abbey. He had slipped the note into a laundry basket being carried up the steps to the front door of Sam's tower by a pair of village girls. It was surely not a monk but a soldier or a servant who could have stopped the girls for a few moments to chat and laugh with them as young men do with girls. But who could it have been? Sam knew of no one next door who sympathized with him, or with the English, or with the Vikings. The source of the message remained a mystery.

However, Sam knew enough about Alonso to believe the message was true. He went at once to the top of his tower and sent three carrier pigeons to Julius the Troll who would send the information on overland to the nearest Vikings—Mordec and his father Hauk—that three ships carrying the Pope's soldiers were on their way to England.

He named the castle that was to be seized. But he knew that the three ships would already have departed, and there was only a very slim chance that Viking reinforcements, starting perhaps from an English base if they had such a thing as yet, could reach the castle in time to warn and guard its people.

As night fell, the three ships approached the English shore soundlessly but for the dipping of the oars. In one of them sat three men who alone of the company wore no armour. They were dressed in the everyday clothes of Vikings, with a sword at their sides and a dagger in their belts.

They were the first to disembark in the shallow bay and wade ashore close to dinner time, their boots hung round their necks. Ahead of them was a forest that would conceal armed men for the next two hours or so.

The three, now booted, and with bulging traders' sacks strapped to their backs, made their way through the trees to a wide clearing. Ahead of them was their destination, a castle with a moat, a closed drawbridge, and no doubt unseen guards on the ramparts. They waited on the edge of the forest screened by the boles of oaks until the moon rose full and bright. Then, led by the tallest of them, they walked towards the castle, visible, unhurried, as three travellers a little tired at the end of a long day.

'Hulloo!' the tall one called. 'Here are three weary travellers begging bed and bread.'

'What is your name? Where do you come from? To where are you bound?' A rough voice replied from high on the wall.

'My name is Kol son of Knefrod. I and my brothers come from trading in London, making our way back north to join our kin.'

A different, quieter voice called 'You are Vikings?'

'We are Vikings, but we come in peace.'

'As Vikings you are welcome here. But let us get a better sight of you.'

The drawbridge came down with a rattle of chains and a low bang as it hit the bank of the moat. The portcullis went up with a series of jerks.

'Enter with your hands in the air,' the harsher voice barked.

Kol son of Knefrod did as he was told, and the other two followed his lead.

They were met by armed men and escorted through a long archway to a large courtyard, where more armed men held up lanterns to inspect their appearance.

'Put down your sacks. Keep your hands from your swords, and come this way.'

They were led into a hall, where the man with the quieter voice stood. 'You say you are Kol son of Knefrod?' he said.

His apparel and rings told Kol that this was the lord of the castle. Beside him stood a lady, her hands folded together inside her blue sleeves which hung almost to her feet.

'That is my name illustrious lord, illustrious lady,' Kol said. 'And these are my two young brothers, Kaal and Kasper.'

As they had been drilled to do, the brothers said in unison: 'Greetings illustrious lord and illustrious lady.'

'Greetings to you, Kaal and Kasper. I am Askr and my wife is Embla. Do these names mean anything to you?'

'Why yes,' said Kol. 'You are named for the first man and the first woman.'

'And do you know why we clothe ourselves in blue garments?'

'In honour of Odin?' Kol said.

Askr laughed. 'Right. You are truly a Viking,' he said. Welcome to our castle, named for the sacred tree.'

'This castle is named Yggdrasil?' Kol raised his eyebrows in mock surprise.

'It is. For we are Vikings too. My wife was born a Viking, and I became one of you by my own choice. See over there on the far wall, between the candles on the wall, Yggdrasil depicted in tapestry. We will regale you and your brothers with the food of Vikings.'

'What is you father's trade?' the Lady Embla asked when they were seated at a table placed in front of a Viking ship displayed in the polished arms of its cradle.

'Our father Knefrod is a hunter. We will be hunters too.'

'I like it when sons follow in their father's trade,' Askr said. 'What were you trading in London?'

'Amber for spices.'

'Put down you sacks and come and sit with us.'

They had only just started to eat and drink, their plates heaped with venison, shark and beans, their cups brimming with ale, when a boy dressed in a white tunic came in with a lyre, sat in the middle of the hall and sang, most beautifully, a song about Odin.

Kol joined in the last few words: '... whose branches reach too high for any man to know where.' He turned to Kaal and Kasper. 'Come on, he said, you should sing it too.' And quickly, seeing that they were at a loss to know what to say, he said to Embla with a smile, 'Their mouths are too happy with your good

food in them to pause from eating merely to sing.'
And Embla smiled back, nodding her understanding
of the appetites of youth.

***

Kol had given his real name to his hosts. But in the
Abbey, and to the officers and most of the men of the
Army of the Redeemed, he was known as Kris—the
name chosen for him by Abbot Alonso. It was to
him that Kol son of Knefrod had come offering his
services against his own people, the Vikings.

'Give me a reason to trust you,' the Abbot had said,
looking suspiciously into the droopy-lidded eyes of
the thin, sallow-faced Viking. Not unapprovingly, the
Abbot assessed him to be a villain. His scalp—shaven
except for a knot of hair on the crown—was crisscrossed with scars. 'Will you accept baptism and so
become one of us?'

'I would be lying if I pretended to believe in your
god,' Kol said. 'Thor has kept me alive in battle.'

'You do not care to lie?' the Abbot said, his eyebrows rising with doubt and surprise.

Kol heard the disbelief in the Christian's tone.

'Not to gods,' he replied, looking down and feeling
his face grow hot.

This was not the first Viking who had ever come
to Alonso offering to serve him, but the first who
refused to be baptized.

'So go on—tell me why I should trust you.'

Kol told the Abbot that he had been cruelly and
unjustly used by his fellow Vikings; rejected, and

51

exiled from his native land, all because he had been falsely accused of treason by one Mordec son of Hauk.

On hearing that name, the Abbot wanted to believe him. There was nobody Alonso longed to have in his power to destroy more than Mordec son of Hauk, who had killed one of his Christians in his own abbey.

But was this Viking telling the truth, the Abbot wondered; or was he sent by the Vikings to tell a false story and become a spy in the army of the Church?

A plan that would test the volunteer and at the same time bring the satisfaction of revenge formed quickly in his mind.

He would use this Viking to lead a raid on the Viking Castle of Yggdrasil. There a search party of his Black Monks had been killed, every one of them to the last man, when they had gone looking for Mordec who—they had been falsely informed—was sheltering there. Now here stood a Viking, a personal enemy of Mordec, surely sent by God for the very purpose of revenge?

***

The true identity of 'Kris' had of necessity been revealed to 'Kaal' and 'Kasper', because he was to lead them as Kol the Viking. Their true names were Arnulf and Denis. They were Christian soldiers willing to pretend to be Vikings. They knew nothing of Viking lore. Kol told them to say as little as possible; to let him do all the talking, and they were happy to obey.

They fully understood that the success of their assignment depended on Kol's winning and keeping the trust of their Viking hosts.

A yellow-liveried serving man led the three of them up winding stairs to a room above the portcullis gate, where a generous heap of straw had been brought for them to sleep on.

After their long day sailing, and food and ale, they would have been glad to sleep. But they did not lie down or close their eyes. They sat still and waited. The castle became quiet but for the sound of the watch patrolling the ramparts.

The moon rose high, bathing the ground with its soft light, as Kol could see through an arrowslit. This night had been chosen by the Abbot because the moon would be full. During the day, as they were sailing, they had often looked up anxiously to see if clouds were forming, and had taken it as a good omen that the sky remained clear.

And their luck held when they were let into the castle, their hosts accepting them as fellow Vikings; and still held when they were shown to quarters just above the castle gate, where, somewhat to their surprise, they were left alone without a single guard sharing the room with them, who would have had to die.

It was plain that they were under no suspicion.

Arnulf and Denis prayed, each silently on his own, that the luck would hold through their dangerous mission.

Kol shook each by a shoulder and led them, barefoot for quietness, down the stairs to the courtyard.

He was ready with a request for a flagon of water if the guards at the gate should notice him too soon. He saw a pair of them standing, lightly armed, facing the entrance arch.

Kol gestured over his shoulder to Arnulf and Denis to advance. The two moved quickly. It was a matter of moments for the unprotected throats of the guards to be slit, and the bodies lowered quietly to the ground.

In the short time that took, Kol had reached the rope-winder beside the portcullis, and started turning it as rapidly as he could. He knew the noise would bring armed men, and the drawbridge had yet to be lowered.

They could hear voices calling, but Arnulf and Denis, well-drilled, were already releasing the chains of the drawbridge from their anchors. They had no intention of running over it when it was down. Out there they would be clear targets for arrows on the open ground in the moonlight. Their plan was to return swiftly up the stairs to the top of the keep.

Kol lifted a lantern from its hook on the wall of the arch, and the three of them reached the foot of the stairs just as armed men came running from doorways round the courtyard.

No one followed them. Safe in their high room, Kol passed the lantern across the arrowslit, back and forth for a minute or more, until he saw men in black armour racing from among the trees towards the castle, some with flaming torches. Would they get to the drawbridge before it was lifted? He tried to hear, through the grow-ing tumult below, through the calls and shouts and blasts on a hunter's horn, the sound of the chains.

But for some reason—bewilderment perhaps, the need to wait for orders perhaps—no one had yet thought of re-sealing the entrance. Perhaps they had only just found the dead bodies and not yet seen the attackers running towards them.

Whatever the reason, luck was still on the raiders' side.

Their trainer had told Kol, Arnulf and Denis that the plan they were to execute was so risky that their chance of survival was small.

Kol was driven to take the risk by his passionate hatred of his fellow Vikings. If he could prove himself now, he would be allowed to enter the fray against them, perhaps even against Mordec himself. It was a chance he had been waiting and hoping for ever since he had had to flee from England with is father after his plot against Mordec had finally failed.

They had found work as mercenary soldiers, once for the Spaniards and three times for the Spaniards' enemies, the Moors. Knefrod the Hunter had fallen in battle, but Kol had been unable to give him a hero's send off to Valhalla.

For all this, resentment consumed him and made him reckless.

Arnulf and Denis had accepted the dangerous mission as soldiers for Christ. They had been chosen for their exceptional piety.

They believed that if they died tonight they would be honoured as Christian martyrs, and maybe even canonized as saints.

Soon whatever could burn inside the stone castle was on fire. The courtyard was full of the black-armoured soldiers who had come thundering over the drawbridge without impediment. The castle guards fought gallantly, and five Christian soldiers had been struck down before others could come up behind them to kill their killers.

The Vikings now understood that this was a revenge attack for their total defeat of a raid by the Black Monks.

They had not been deceived then, when the armed monks said they had come only to parley, as they were in search of one Viking only—Mordec son of Hauk. They had let the warrior monks in, and slaughtered them with boiling pitch, swords, clubs and battleaxes.

Now they were the losers. At the end of an hour or so, there was not a single inhabitant of the Castle Yggdrasil left alive. They lay in the blood of their wounds, or suffocated by smoke in their chambers, both men and women.

On a bed of white furs, untouched by sword or dagger, lay the Lady Embla, choked in her sleep by the thick fumes. Askr lay on the grass of the courtyard, his blue robe soaked purple with his blood, his fingers chopped off for the rings they had worn.

Kol, Arnulf and Denis survived to fight another day; Kol and Denis without a scratch on them, and Arnulf with nothing worse than a bruised foot which had been caught briefly in a loop of the heavy drawbridge chain.

Denis told Kol that they were alive and well because he had prayed and Christ had protected them.

No one came to find them in the tower. They descended when they heard their fellow soldiers singing a hymn of thanks to the Lord God, 'The God of Battles', for their victory.

Arnulf, wandering about, came upon the boy musician. He lay in his white tunic face down before a tapestry of Yggdrasil, the Vikings' Tree of Life, his arms spread out as though in supplication, his throat slit from ear to ear.

And near him lay two dead Christians with their necks broken.

the vikings depart

In the pearly light of a very early summer morning, the great Viking fleet was set to sail, each ship starting soon after midnight to receive its contingent of armed men eager for battle.

The day and hour had been decided as soon as the commanders knew the plans of the enemy, relayed to them from Sam of the West through Julius the Troll.

They would be waiting on English soil for the landing of the Pope's army.

Leif woke soon after midnight in his corner of the stable.

He rose quietly, hoping not to waken Eyrin. The evening before, when Eyrin had gone to bed, and Hauk, Estrid and Mordec were talking about the departure and how Estrid could manage the farm and the mead-making with the help of the bondsmen for as long as the war would last ('four months at most,' Hauk had reckoned), Leif had said: 'I would like to help you, Eyrin's mother, but I am going with Mordec.'

He had expected a chorus of objections, but Hauk and Estrid said nothing, only looked at Mordec as though this was a matter that concerned him alone.

Mordec had stared thoughtfully at Leif for a few moments, and then, 'Yes' he had said. 'Yes, you will

come with me.' And he'd smiled as he added, 'I happen to have a suit of armour which I've grown out
of and I think we can reduce in size a bit more to
fit you.'

'And can I have a sword?'

'Yes. You can. You can have a sword.'

'Some of the other boys say they'll sail in the small
ship Foal of the Foam, towed by one of the big ships,
but I want to be in the same ship with you.'

'You'll be with me in Harald Goldmountain's ship.
He asked Dad and me to sail with him. I don't think
he'll mind if you come too. And Foal of the Foam
will *not* be sailing.'

Leif had been so excited he'd found it hard to get
to sleep, and he had not slept long. Now, quiet as he
tried to be putting on his clothes, something caused
Eyrin to stir and open his eyes.

'What are you doing?' the little boy asked. 'Why
are you getting dressed so early? Where are you
going?'

Those were just the questions Leif had hoped not
to have to answer. He guessed they would lead to
protest and maybe even tears.

There was no way to give Eyrin his answer other
than simply and plainly, no sense in trying to sweeten
it, and no point in deferring it.

'I'm going with Mordec.'

'To England? To the war?'

Leif nodded.

'I don't want you to go. I want you to stay with
me.'

'Mordec wants me to go with him. He said so last night.'

'No. You mustn't go. You could get killed.'

'I won't get killed. Mordec will look after me. He has to. He must do what I say, because he belongs to me. You remember I told you how a magician brought him to me when I was in a strange land and I wanted a Viking friend?'

'Don't I belong to you too?'

'We belong to each other.'

'Then don't go. I don't want you to go.'

'Your mother will bring you to the ships. You can watch the army embark and the fleet depart. It will be grand.'

'I don't want you to go!'

There was a quaver in Eyrin's voice, and Leif feared that tears were coming.

'We are Vikings, Eyrin,' he said sternly. 'We are brave. We face what we don't like with courage. We don't complain about it.'

Eyrin swallowed hard.

'Well, I'm getting up now. I'll come and … watch the ships sail.'

'That's right. That's good. That's brave. You'll wave to me. Mordec and I will wave to you. You will smile. If you cry you will make your mother unhappy. But I know that you will make her as proud of you as she is of us.'

While they were breakfasting on bacon, eggs and pomegranates, a messenger arrived from Julius the Troll, one of his dwarfs dressed in red.

He had galloped all the way to their gate on a small but very strong horse, and he had run from the gate to the house, and now he was too breathless to deliver his message.

'Something urgent?' Hauk had asked as the dwarf stood panting.

He nodded, and finally puffed out: 'Urgent, yes. Huh. From Sam. Huh. Of the West. Huh. A hundred men. Huh. Of the Pope's army. Huh. Sent ahead to England. Huh. To take the Viking Castle of Yggdrasil.'

Julius the Troll had instructed him to speak the message first, then to hand over a letter which would tell the Vikings more.

Hauk read the letter speedily and handed it to Mordec, who rose at once and rushed out the door. He made for the gate, not the stable, deciding it would be quicker for him to run than fetch a horse, saddle it, and ride to the shipyard where the Commander's men would likely be assembling now.

When he reached the main road it was full of armed men making their way to the harbour, women and children among them, and babies in the arms of their mothers. He weaved his way through them, jostling them, apologizing, but never stopping until he saw the Commander in the distance, clear enough under the soft light of the white sky.

Commander Tostig stood on the top step of the shipyard office, a crowd about him, more coming to join it every moment and some hurrying off to carry out orders. Tostig son of Tostig was a distinctive figure, tall and broad. His brown hair hung straight over his ears; his beard was cut straight across. He was not yet in his armour, but was dressed in a dark blue tunic and cloak.

Mordec began to wave and shout to get his attention as soon as he saw him. But Tostig, trying to hear many voices all calling out at once, only became aware of Mordec as he pushed his way through the crowd. When he saw the young man approaching, urgency written on his face and his determined advance, squeezing between men in chainmail with swords at their sides, he thought at once, 'Here's trouble coming.' But he was not a man to be easily perturbed.

Mordec stopped on the lowest of the six steps, looking up at the Commander, and found himself in the same plight as the dwarf when he had needed to deliver the same urgent message. But he took one deep breath, and blurted out, 'Illustrious Commander, the Pope has sent an advance unit to England to take the Viking Castle of Yggdrasil.'

The crowd around him fell silent. Tostig raised a hand and shouted, 'Hear!' and even the more distant cries and chatter stopped.

Tostig had heard every word that Mordec had so rapidly delivered.

'When?' Tostig demanded. 'When did they sail, from what port and how many?'

'A hundred. Two days ago. From the southernmost port of Normandy. Three men to enter the castle as travellers then to let the main force in. For a Christian command centre for the war.'

Now Tostig bent a little towards Mordec and asked him to repeat the message slowly, which Mordec did, and he held out the letter. Tostig straightened up and beckoned with both hands. 'Come up here,' he said.

When Mordec stood beside the Commander, his head was nearly on a level with the man's, and his face was being searched by a pair of light blue eyes.

'You must be Mordec, who fought the Cid in Italy, and reigned as a prince in Cum-ree?'

'My name is Mordec, yes, illustrious Commander. Mordec son of Hauk.'

'I've heard tell of you, of course, Mordec son of Hauk. And you are the only Viking I have seen in years who looks at the world through his own private windows.'

'But about the Castle of Yggdrasil …' Mordec said, trying to sound respectful while agitated because time was being spent without action.

Tostig read the letter and Mordec watched his face anxiously. When the Commander looked up he put a hand on Mordec's shoulder. 'If they have already sailed we cannot get reinforcements to the castle in time to save it. We have none now in England that we can dispatch. If the castle is sacked and taken and the Vikings killed, all we can do is avenge them,' he said. '*And that we will do*, I promise you, Mordec.'

That was all he intended to say at that time about the bad news. He turned away to see to more pressing concerns. Mordec descended the steps, returned to the road, and struggled back through the still advancing crowd, this time against its flow, making slow progress until he reached the narrow road to his own house. His feelings were mixed. He was happy and proud to know that the Commander had heard of him, and that they had spoken to each other man to man. But at the same time he felt anger and regret that the first battle of this war was probably already lost to his personal enemy, the Abbot Alonso de Llama.

An hour later, he and Hauk and Leif were on their way to the harbour, followed by Estrid and Eyrin, who was holding her hand tightly, and behind them came bondsmen pushing their baggage on handcarts.

The main road was less crowded now. Most of the soldiers would be in their ships, their wives and children lined up along the quay, on the beaches, on the cliffs, to see the biggest Viking fleet that had ever assembled on this part of the coast sail westward to war.

The priest would be standing on the edge of the cliff calling upon Thor to strengthen every man, and nobody ('not even Thor,' Mordec said to Leif) would be listening to him.

Leif's eyes were alight with excitement. The armour Mordec had worn when he'd raided England had been taken apart and partially put together again to cover his smaller chest and back. He had no boots, but Estrid had polished his shoes to the same brightness as Mordec's boots. A short sword hung from his belt, and Mordec had promised to teach him how to use it.

He was still a little surprised that Mordec and the grown-ups had so easily agreed to let him go to this war. He wondered if they had some reason they were not telling him.

Not that it mattered. All that mattered was that he was going with Mordec, with the army, and—what was more—in the biggest and best ship in the harbour, the one that belonged to Harald Goldmountain. Leif held the very big man in awe, and would have thought him scary if he didn't often, suddenly, laugh like a happy god.

And here came the great man now, sober and serious today, seated on the high bench draped and cushioned in purple. He was robed in purple, and diamonds flashed on his fingers. His pale horses pulled the chariot along, driven by Bernie who sat on the drivers' seat clothed and turbaned all in white, his feet bare as always but his legs sheathed in purple leather.

Drummers and pipers followed, playing not martial music but sweet tunes. They were followed by cooks and servants, the men in armour, the women in white, all of them singing softly to the tune of the drums and flutes.

Last came the slaves bearing the bags, bundles, and barrels that would accompany Harald on his voyage and keep him comfy for a good while in England. (The slaves, the women, and the horses would not sail with him but be returned to Hedeby under the supervision of the older grooms. There were plenty of slaves, women, and horses in England.)

Ships were already being rowed out of the harbour to join the main body of the waiting fleet, when Harald Goldmountaun stepped down from his chariot on to the quay.

He strode straight to where the meadmaker and his family stood waiting for his arrival, He did not seize Estrid in his arms and lift her this time, but took her hand and bowed over it respectfully.

Still holding her hand on his palm he straightened and said, 'Illustrious Lady Estrid! You and your husband lent me your house, your bed, and the companionship of your extraordinary son. I thank you. I want to return good for good. I do nothing that is not for my own benefit, but I like it best when the benefit I get from others is also of benefit to them. That is good commerce. I have left something, under the pillow on the bed where I slept so well, for you to find when we are gone. I hope it will gladden your heart.'

He turned away to face the retinue he was leaving behind, raised both arms above his head and cried out, 'Let the war begin!'

The crowd of women and children and old men on the quay, the drummers and pipers, the servants and slaves responded with a roar and a crash into music. Which made Harald Goldmountain fling back his head and laugh his enormous laugh. And everyone laughed with him, the crowd on the quay, the crew on the ship, and Hauk and Estrid, Mordec and Leif, and most of all, in sheer delight at so much happiness, little Eyrin. The great guffaw was followed by a chortle and the chortle by the series of hoots that ended with another chortle.

The crowd cheered. Harald waved with both hands, both arms. The cheering went on as he climbed the ladder to his ship, closely followed by Bernie who held his Master's shoulders to keep him steady. When Harald's foot touched the deck, the crew whistled and clapped.

Hauk, Mordec and Leif took their baggage off the cart. Most of the bags were Mordec's. In addition to his personal things, his armour and weapons and fishing-rods, he was taking his maps and needed books. Leif lifted the bag of books with some difficulty. Hauk took it from him. He and Mordec each made two trips between the cart and the deck of the ship before everything was on board. Then the three voyagers embraced Estrid and Eyrin one last time and took themselves up the ladder.

Harald's ship, by far the largest in the fleet, was one of only ten drawn up beside the quay. A hundred small boats, rowed by boys just too young to serve in the army, had borne the soldiers to the other ships. Many of these little craft bobbed on the water beyond the harbour wall as the boys watched the fleet bear their fathers and brothers away.

Now the old priest who stood on the cliff above the harbour began to sing, in a reedy voice, an invocation to Thor asking for victory, but still nobody took any notice of him.

One by one the last ten ships were pushed out, and when they were clear of the quay, oars were lifted and worked at once in perfect unison. The men sat looking rigidly forward, their helmets on, their shields hung along the sides of the vessels. None looked back. None waved. Their military obedience had begun. There was no sense in calling out to them, they would not respond. So the women and children stood silently watching them depart. Some of the children waved but expected no response.

The priest came down from the cliff and went home to a late breakfast.

The second last ship to leave bore the Commander. All the attention of the watchers was on him now, Tostig son of Tostig who would lead the army to victory. He stood beside the mast, one arm extended in the direction the mighty force of the Vikings was to sail. When his craft was in front of all the others, the rest started after him. He would stand there until the shore was out of sight, pointing until his arm ached and dropped to his side, after which his nose would point the way.

Last to leave was Harald Goldmountain's huge white ship, Pearl of the Deep. Her sail was made of wide stripes alternating purple and white. Her mast was gilded. Harald himself sat in her bows on a gilded chair under a canopy of purple silk. Bernie stood behind him.

As Pearl of the Deep was not under military command, her passengers were free to wave to the watchers on the shore. Hauk, Mordec and Leif waved, and Estrid and Eyrin waved back.

Eyrin went on waving long after the three faces were lost in the distance and Pearl of the Deep herself was only a flash of gold as the top of her mast caught a ray of the brightening sun.

captain anwid
catches the drift

'Can you assure me that you and your daughters are baptized Christians?'

'I have always understood that I was christened,' replied Botham, Earl of Felldown. 'What I don't understand is why they christened me Botham. That name proved to be somewhat of a curse, I can tell you, when I was a boy. The other boys called me Bummy, you see, which I felt was quite unnecessarily rude. But I didn't want them to know that I resented it, so I got the idea of *calling myself* Bummy. That took the sting out of it, if you see what I mean.'

'And your daughters?' Abbot Alonso de Llama turned his head (which was crowned with a circle of fair curls round the pink disc of a monk's tonsure), towards the two women who sat, side by side opposite the Earl, at an oak table in the old Roman house known as Cogg Hall. Presumably he was looking at the women, but as he kept his eyelids lowered, no one could be quite sure.

'My daughters?' the Earl queried. 'I do have a daughter, a very fine gel, and here she is. Her name is Anwid.'

'The Lady Anwid—' Alonso began, but was interrupted by the lady herself.

'*Captain* Anwid is the title I prefer.'

'Captain Anwid,' the Abbot started again, 'and I are acquainted. I had the honour of receiving her at my Abbey. Furthermore, she is a person of renown. Captain, would you set my mind at rest by assuring me that you too received the sacrament of baptism?'

'As far as I know, yes, I did. I have always understood that I was christened here in our own church.'

'I would be grateful of you would show me you church by and by. And your sister—'

'Oh, we are not sisters,' the Captain said, 'This is Charlotte the dancer, Charlotte the mummer, famous throughout the whole world. Surely you've heard of her?'

'You should see the gel dance—the Earl began, but cut himself short. 'No, maybe not.'

'Mistress Charlotte,' Alonso persisted. 'Have you been redeemed? By baptism? Are you a Christian?'

Charlotte rose from her chair, dropped a curtsey to the Abbot, then turned away from him. A moment later she whirled round, and now in her arms lay a bundle like a swaddled baby. Where she had got it from her three watchers could not guess.

She sat down, rocking the baby gently. The baby started crying. Charlotte's lips did not move, yet the baby cried 'Wha-whaa-whaa!'

'Sh!' said the mother of the bundle as she rocked and rocked the crying child.

But the baby cried, 'Wha-whaa-whaaa!'

The mother raised one hand towards the beams of the roof, looking up raptly as if at a vision, nodded, dipped the hand into an imaginary font, shook off some drops of water, and made the cross on the head of the crying bundle. At once the baby stopped crying.

Charlotte folded her arms. The baby had disappeared.

Alonso frowned. Was this witchcraft? But as the Earl and the Captain started laughing with delight at the clever performance, and Charlotte herself sat demurely with a candid expression on her innocent young face, the Abbot dismissed his suspicion and merely said, 'Thank you, Mistress, for your answer. You remind me of my silent contest with my neighbour Sam of the West, the fame of which has spread throughout the world. I think you meant to—am I right?'

Charlotte nodded.

'And you leave it to me to put your answer into words. You know the comfort of baptism as a baby knows the comfort of its mother's love. Am I right?'

Charlotte nodded again.

'Then I have only one more question to ask before you take me to see your church. Do you pray? Do all of you pray?'

'Plenty of praying has gone on here. Plenty, in its day,' said the Earl. 'We even had a priest here for a time. Cornelius was his name.'

'What happened to him?' the Abbot enquired.

'He vanished. One day he was here, and the next he was gone.'

'How long ago was that?'

'Oh, fifteen years ago, give or take a month or two. Do you know—it was the darnedest thing—my wife disappeared on the very same day. Not heard a word from either of them since.'

'Your wife?' For a moment the Abbot's eyes were to be seen, violet-blue, as his lids opened wide in surprise. But they were quickly lowered again.

'Not having him here will be a bother when Anwid gets married, which will be quite soon now. We'll have to send for a priest from London, probably.'

'You are to be married soon, Captain?'

'It's Father's wish,' Anwid said.

'I would be delighted to officiate—' the Abbot began.

'But there's a bit of a hitch,' Anwid said, raising her voice. 'I haven't yet found a husband.'

'Oh she will.' the Earl said. 'I know how these things are done. I will hold a ball, and young men will come from all over England, and she will give her hand to the lucky one, and then in due course I will have a grandson to inherit Felldown and Cogg Hall.'

The Earl and Anwid took the Abbot to inspect their church, a low brick structure with a high bell-tower, built on a grassy knoll where once a Roman fane had stood. Anwid carried the big iron key to the double oak doors which, like the sturdy bell-tower, seemed too good to be part of the shed-like building itself. The key was rusty and hard to turn, but Anwid's strong hands mastered it.

'What is this?' the Abbot asked, stopping still as soon as he stepped inside, gesturing at the objects leaning against the walls and lying on the pews. He picked up a short plank of smooth wood with a handle attached to it.

'We store a few things back here,' Anwid said hurriedly. 'We don't use these things much any more, but we did when Cornelius was here. *Father* Cornelius, I mean. That's a bat for the game of creckett. The farm boys and I used to play it. And these were our fishing rods and nets, and these were hurdles we used to jump over. Father Cornelius taught the boys to read and write. He was a really good priest, Reverend Sir. He taught them to read the bible. Yes. And look, down here, the altar is made of oak, and the crucifix was hand-carved by our own carpenter, an excellent craftsman. Father Cornelius kept everything dusted and polished. But it's been some time now …'

She did not usually make excuses. She cared little what people thought of her. But she had reason to keep the rather unfriendly Abbot as friendly as she could.

He had arrived that morning on their shore in a ship as full of Black Monks as of soldiers. As the Army of the Redeemed was expected to reach England on this day, she had posted the all-girl crew of her missing ship on the dunes. As soon as they spotted the red sail with the white cross, they had sent her word, and she was on the beach to meet the troops she expected would land. But there was only one ship, and only the Abbott himself and three of his monks came ashore.

It was a still, warm, cloudless day. The Captain and the Abbot greeted each other with all due courtesy. The three monks, their black hoods pulled so far forward that their faces were in deep shadow, stood behind him, meekly looking down at the pebbles and shale. The Abbot was more comfortably dressed in a dark red tunic and a matching cloak with a large white cross on its back. As another sign of his calling he wore a wooden cross hanging on a cord from his thin leather belt.

'We have no violent intentions towards good Christians or their property,' the Abbot said at once. 'It is to protect them that we have come. Our enemies are the heathens. We will cleanse England of them, either by expelling them or by converting them. Better by converting them, of course. We will presume upon your hospitality for a few hours, dear lady, while I make enquiry if there be any heathen on your land. Please permit these three experienced inquisitors of mine to question your serfs—'

'We have no serfs,' Anwid corrected him. 'all our tenants are freeborn Englishmen and women.'

'Apologies. To question your tenants, I should say. If we have find no reason to fear that your land will become a haven for the enemy, or harbour spies and informers, we will ask nothing of you but to purchase food from your farms. The camp for the troops that are to follow will be set up outside your border. And we will expect you to let us know if the enemy approaches you.'

'I am not the lord of Felldown, Reverend Sir. It is my father who must come to any agreement with you. I will take you to him.'

'And my monks may seek out your tenants and question them, and give them their instructions?'

Anwid did not care to have a stranger give instructions to their tenants, but she caught the menace in the Abbot's voice. Menace was the note his character was tuned to. She had learnt that on her first encounter with him. His demand was clear without being spoken: '*Do as I say, and you will not be harmed; disobey, and we will take all you have and destroy you.*'

'Of course,' she said. 'your people have the freedom of our estate. For whatever time they need.'

One of the Black Monks came to the little church just as she, her father and the Abbot were leaving it. The Abbot instructed him to 'clear the church of all that does not belong in it', and to 'test the bell rope and the bell'. He plainly believed that the church—any church—came under his rule. But why the testing of the bell-rope and the bell? She asked the Abbot this, and he replied:

'The soldiers will be instructed to stay off your property unless they are summoned by the bell. If word reaches us that you have been troubled by enemy intruders, a monk will come and ring your Church bell to alert the men. I would advise you not to resist if it comes to that, Captain Anwid. Your tenants and servants will be no match for the Army of the Redeemed.'

Anwid was not thinking of the tenants and servants. She was wondering how much of a resistance to an invasion, whether of the Redeemed or the Vikings, she and her crew could put up. Her girls would fight valiantly, she knew, but they would be greatly outnumbered.

The Abbot bowed farewell to his host, thanked him rather elaborately for his 'noble hospitality', and started back towards the shore.

Anwid accompanied him.

'I myself,' he told her, 'will not be here often with my monks. Today I return to the Abbey. I am the Commander-in-Chief, but the officers on the ground will decide how to carry out the great plan His Holiness the Pope and I have devised. I may appear unannounced from time to time. My monks will be lodging at the mission just north of your border near the town of Dorobrevis. They will take turns keeping a watch on your property. Reinforcements for our soldiers will come from the south, from the Castle of Yggdrasil. We took it from the Vikings four days ago, did you know? They paid heavily for resistance. Sadly, none of them survived. Did you hear about that?'

The menace in his voice was undisguised now.

'I did,' she replied.

'We must not feel too doleful for those who fell. A few months ago they slaughtered without mercy a peaceful contingent of my Black Monks who had sought their hospitality while on a special mission. Have you heard about *that*?'

'Mm-hmm,' Anwid murmured.

'They were searching, my monks were, for a particular Viking. You know him. He was a passenger on your ship. I am sure you were aware that he killed one of my Christians in cold blood? He should never have been allowed to sail away from the island on your ship—had you known.'

Anwid said nothing.

'Let me remind you of his name, Captain. So if he comes to you for asylum, you will know to get word to my people at Dorobrevis. Mordec son of Hauk is his name. You remember him, of course?'

'Of course. He was left on my ship when the rest of us were taken captive by Bjarwulf the Pirate. I think he may not have survived.'

'Oh, he survived,' Alonso said. 'He will come to England to fight in this war. He may very well seek you out.'

'I'm glad he is alive,' Anwid said. 'How do you know?'

Alonso knew by his continuing desire for vengeance; but he did not say so, and Anwid guessed it and did not press him to reply.

'I see no reason why he should seek me out,' she said.

They walked on in silence for a while. As they came to the dunes, where her girls were still standing in a wide half-circle facing the beach, their quivers on their backs, their bows resting beside them, the Abbot said quietly, gazing into the blue distance; 'I am told it was the King of Cornwall who told my men that Mordec son of Hauk was to be found at the Castle Yggdrasil.'

Anwid said nothing.

'I believe you are related to the King of Cornwall?'

She caught his drift.

'We are cousins,' Anwid confessed.

'I cannot help wondering whether he was merely mistaken, or whether he intended to deceive my monks.'

Anwid slightly shook her head. This sort of talk was against her instinct. Candid by nature, she would rather an accuser challenge her outright and she reply with the truth. She preferred to fight with weapons than spar with weasel words.

'I have also been told,' Alonso went on in his quiet, sinister way, 'that you, dear lady, were visiting him on his island at the time.'

'I have visited King Mark on his island.'

'But you know nothing of his motive in giving my monks the misdirection?'

The Abbot's meaning was not hard to interpret. *'I know that you were there. I know that you are implicated in the plot that destroyed my monks. I have you at my mercy now. I will bide my time for revenge. Meanwhile, if you hope to assuage me, do nothing to offend me or my wrath will descend thunderously on you and yours.'*

They had reached the edge of the sea. He had been seen approaching and a small boat had been sent to meet him. The oarsman had pulled it halfway out of the water and was standing patiently beside it a few yards ahead.

The Abbot stopped and turned to face Anwid.

'Farewell, Captain. Farewell, my child. May God keep you.'

He hurriedly made the sign of the cross over her head, and walked away.

He did not look back. She watched him sitting in the small boat looking out to sea. She watched him climb a rope ladder; watched the oarsman do the same; watched the small boat being hauled up to the deck; and she watched the ship depart. Its rowers and a sweet breeze took it smoothly out of the bay. She watched the red sail with the white cross on it move out of sight round the headland.

'It was the boatmen!' she said to herself. 'Of course. They returned to the Abbey when they gave up waiting for the Black Monks to come back from the castle of Yggdrasil. They took the tale that it was King Mark who sent them to their doom, telling them Mordec was sheltering there. They picked up the gossip that I was visiting the King. And when Alonso heard that, he guessed it was I, *not* the King, who had known what awaited his Black Monks. He *knows* it was I who sent them to their certain deaths.'

She waved to her crew to come to her on the beach. The noise of the breaking waves would keep her voice from carrying far. From now on she would be careful what she said, to whom, and where.

'We will not be able to defend Cogg Hall,' she told her warrior girls. 'We will be hugely outnumbered. Cogg Hall will be lost to us. Felldown will be lost to us. The Earl must go away soon. And we will go and join the English army, as I promised Queen Lily we would. We'll fight with her—against both the Vikings *and* the Pope's army. Are you willing?'

They all nodded.

'When do we start?' asked Dellibeth, the lean strong redhead who usually spoke for them all.

'Can't say right now. Be ready to leave at any time.'

'Aye, aye, Captain,' the girls said, and off they marched, bows over their shoulders, in single file to their barracks.

'What I must do now is—first, persuade father he must go to Cornwall, to shelter with his cousin the King,' Anwid said to the breeze, as she started up the path over the dunes. 'That could be the hardest part.'

a quiet and easy conquest

The Viking fleet divided when the leading ships came within sight of the English coast. About a third of them sailed north-west for an hour and anchored in a deep-water bay with a five-ship harbour. The others, led by the Commander's ship, sailed south-west to the mouth of the river that bore the Viking name of Nijn.

Its delta embraced many small marshy islands. At the point upstream where the river itself narrowed, they had their landing stage and a long-established settlement. Mordec knew that country well, having lived there for a season and come close to death in one of its bogs. He himself did not go there—he was among those who sailed north—but his maps of the region lay rolled up in the Commander's seachest.

Pearl of the Deep rocked gently on little waves in the deep-water bay. It was a warm day. Harald lay in a hammock, covered with a light sheet, while Bernie, wearing only a loin-cloth and turban, stood beside him and stirred the air around his Master's face with a fan made of tail-feathers plucked from white peacocks.

Mordec was not observing them. He was simultaneously teaching Leif how to use his sword, and watching an invasion begin in accordance with the Commander's orders.

The invasion was starting with a single officer approaching a closed gate.

One of the five ships tied up along the quay was a Viking ship. The captain, Trygve son of Ivar, had just disembarked with three of his soldiers, and they were walking along the quay. He was a heavy man, not young but muscular. His sheathed sword hung at his side, but he was not wearing helmet or body-armour. He stopped at a gate in a high wooden fence. The other three disappeared among trees at the end of the quay.

Mordec, while easily parrying a sudden thrust by Leif, saw Captain Trygve pull the bell-rope beside the gate.

A monk in a black habit, the hood laid back so that his face and head—a tonsure wreathed with ginger hair—were plain to see, opened the gate and smiled a pleasant greeting. Stepping aside, he gestured a welcoming invitation to the visitor to enter. Captain Trygve walked into the grounds of Barleyfield Monastery, the monk closed the gates, and Mordec turned his attention back to swordplay. He would have to wait to know the next move in the war.

He knew what the Commander had in mind for this Christian establishment. He wanted to take it without violence and make it one of his command headquarters. Mordec trusted Tostig, but at the same time felt some tension as he thought about the possibility that a battle might be about to ensue here, in the Commander's absence.

Sooner or later, of course, Leif would have to see battle; see how fiercely Vikings fought; see blood; see killing. But not yet. He wanted Leif to remain here under the protection of Hauk when he himself went south where hot battle would soon be raging.

After barely half an hour had passed, Captain Trygve opened the gate himself and walked out on to the quay, leaving the gate open. He entered his own ship, and soon two small boats were lowered from it, a messenger in each.

They went from ship to ship across the bay, giving instructions to the captains.

One of them came at last to Pearl of the Deep. He did not come aboard, but called up to Mordec: 'Greetings from Captain Trygve to the illustrious lord, Harald Goldmountain. He will come himself to report on the surrender of the enemy.'

When, some time later, the Captain came aboard Pearl of the Deep, Harald, Mordec and Hauk heard how very quietly and easily the monastery had been captured, or 'subdued' as the Captain joked.

'I was taken straight to the Abbot as I commanded. As soon as he saw me he started talking, saying he had been expecting us, and when he saw our ships arriving he had instructed his monks to be welcoming, because we were welcome, very welcome to whatever they had, there was ample room for all of us to live together with them in peace. And without taking another breath, his words tumbling over themselves, he told me that he would not allow the Pope's soldiers to be billeted here and they themselves were not armed and there were no weapons anywhere in the monastery and I could have the place searched as thoroughly as I cared to and all his monks were at my disposal to meet all my wishes. His face was red, his hands were clasped like this, and he stuttered a bit. I could tell he was afraid. I just stood and listened to him until he finished. Then he smiled. You should have seen his smile. It was so forced. It looked like this.'

Trygve's imitation of the abbot's smile was overdone but funny. Harald burst into his great laugh, and everyone—except Bernie, who was carefully pouring wine into crystal goblets—laughed too.

The rest of the account of the quiet conquest was soon told. The abbot's hope that meekness, submission, and generosity would keep his monks in the monastery even if they had to share it with Vikings, was disappointed.

Captain Trygve smiled back at the abbot, and asked him, 'Do you have ample stores of food?'

'Oh yes,' said the abbot.

'Do you have a cool place stocked with excellent wine and ale?'

'Oh yes,' said the abbot.

'Good. I give you one hour to leave,' the Captain said, still speaking softly, almost sweetly. 'Every last one of you. Take nothing with you but the garments on your backs and the sandals on your feet.'

'He didn't smile at that?' Hauk guessed.

'He did not. The smile vanished in a split second.'
The Captain demonstrated the smile suddenly going,
and Harald laughed again, even luder. This time they
could hear men who had been left on watch on the
other ships joining the laughter as Harald's roar of
delight rang out across the bay.

The Captain went on with his tale.

'He asked if they could take bread with them for
the journey. I said no. "Then may we take our begging bowls?" he said. "Yes." I said, "you may." No one
can say we treated them badly. They go unharmed.
And they'll go as far from us as they can. I saw most of
them heading north. My look-outs spotted three of
them hurrying in the other direction—southwards,
taking the news of their loss to the Pope's army, of
course. They weren't quick and they weren't quiet,
though I think they meant to be. They'll have to find
horses—of the land or the sea—or the war will be
over before they get to tell their tale.'

'Are their stores as ample as the abbot said?' Hauk
asked him.

'They are. We'll all dine well tonight at their ex-
pense, and sleep in their beds.'

Mordec's orders were to make maps of the territory, so he chose a room with high and wide windows
to let in the light. Leif, poking about in chests and
cupboards, found a long silver cross.

'Look at the funny swords they use, Mordec. It's
hard to hold the handle because its sort of square. And
it's got no point—it couldn't make a hole in a pillow.
If they use things like this, we'll win for sure.'

Mordec explained what it was. 'They nailed a man on it?' Leif repeated, pulling a face.

'We too nail men onto poles,' Mordec said. 'But only after we've killed them in war.'

the angels of the nijn

The Viking warships were flat-bottomed, designed to be carried over land and sailed along shallow rivers when necessary. So how the fleet disappeared in the wide mouth of the River Nijn* is no real mystery.

The Vikings themselves, waiting in unpolished steel helmets and dark chain mail on the myriad islands of the delta, were also invisible to the Christian invaders when the deep-bottomed ships arrived at that part of the English coast.

It looked to the Christians to be deserted. But it was perilous for them beyond their worst fears.

In small boats they came, rowing up the river and exploring here and there the waterways between the islands. The Vikings let them get far upstream, then closed behind them, cutting them off from retreat. Never suspecting that they were being watched and out-manoeuvred, platoons of heavily armed but lightly armoured men climbed up both banks of the river and walked, wary and doomed, deeper and deeper into the trap the Vikings had set for them. White crosses on red tunics were invitations to the Viking bowmen, but they shot not a single arrow as they awaited the word of command.

---

* Pronounced 'Neen'

Only when the first unit of the leading Christian brigade, now with even more caution, approached the silent, apparently abandoned Viking settlement, and began to look into the empty houses, did Commander Tostig, crouched with his force in the shallow marsh behind their backs, rise with a cry of 'Attack!' to lead a rush of warriors who, screaming like seagulls, fell upon the startled Christians with such fury that many were paralyzed with fea and could not raise their weapons.

The when the Viking battle-axes descended on their backs, their half-shielded faces, their arms and legs, they found their assailants too close to be struck or pierced with swords.

At the same time, the rest of the Viking army, spread out along the marshy lands beside the river and all over the islands of the delta, sprang into action. Vikings appeared on all sides of the Christian soldiers, along the river banks, among the reeds at the edges of the islands, up through the mud of the marshes, out of the very air it would seem, before them, behind them, on top of them.

The Army of the Redeemed was young, with few experienced fighters in it. They had all been in training for more than a year, but not for what they now encountered. Many fought bravely, and some fought well, but they were up against seasoned professional fighters.

They knew at once that their struggle was hopeless.

Long since persuaded to have faith in the power of prayer, they all prayed, or called upon their Lord

God, aloud or silently, as the killing blows came down upon them.

In that battle, which was to become famous as the Battle of the Nijn, the Christian force was massacred. The Vikings took no prisoners. As one fell wounded, his Viking attacker finished him off. The noise of the battle, the shouts, shrieks, grunts, cries, bird-calls, and the grate of steel on steel, went on for hours.

One of Tostig's officers was killed, run through by the sword of a Christian whose own head was struck off a moment later with one blow by Tostig himself. Seven other Vikings were killed, and forty gravely wounded. The Viking dead were lain aside with reverence. They would be given the funeral rites of heroes when the battle was over.

Most of the Christian dead were tipped into the water, but a good many were kept for a customary use of enemy corpses that was almost as sacred to the Vikings as the ritual with which they honoured their own fallen warriors.

By the time the dark came down, there was a fire on every island, and on the lurid colour of flame the bodies of Christians were illuminated. Each was raised high on an upended oar; his torso was slit from throat to groin; his rib cage wrenched open and spread wide so that the two sides looked like the wings of angels painted on the walls of their churches—except that the 'feathers' were rib-bones. At their first glimpse of one such 'angel', the Christian crews on the waiting ships seized their oars, raised their sails, and fled from the fiery, blood-soaked, gruesome shore. A few survivors of Alonso's doomed platoons had reached the ships before they sailed, all of them wounded and some dying.

When the invader was gone, the Viking dead were brought to the sea, each in a small boat. The warrior lay in his armour, on his back, with his arms crossed. His sword was placed on his body, the hilt under his chin, and his axe and dagger on either side of his helmeted head. His boat was set on fire and pushed out to sea.

The tide took it, rocking and burning, while the soul of the hero rose through the Milky Way to Valhalla, where Odin greeted him by his name, and all the gods shouted it. There he would live and feast among the gods and heroes forever.

Boat after boat, fourteen in all, drifted flaming on the sea, under the black sky diamonded with stars.

Vikings on the shore, stained and filthy with the blood and mud of battle, watched wearily until day-break made the burning boats invisible.

Then they embraced each other and laughed, because they were alive and victorious.

a gift but if …

Estrid supposed that the gift Harald Goldmountain had left under a pillow might be a gemstone.

'A pearl perhaps,' she murmured to herself, perhaps because the name of Harald's ship—Pearl of the Deep—on which her husband and son were on their way to war, was in her thoughts.

But what she found when she lifted the pillow was, to her surprise, a scroll.

And what she found written on the scroll was a much greater surprise.

'Illustrious lady Esther Estrid daughter of Adam. I have chosen your son Mordec to be my heir. As I am childless and will not marry again, I have for some time been looking about me for a young man who will carry on my works when I die. I heard of Mordec because I was told the skalds recite a saga about him. But all that they say he has done would not make him a good manager. Heroes are not often fit for daily work and the care of money. So I asked your father if Mordec could work with numbers and manage an estate. He said he could, and I believe him because he is always truthful. He would not make up cause for praise just because Mordec is his grandson. Still I needed to meet Mordec myself. So

I chose your home to stay in while I waited to go
to war. You know now that I love and esteem him.
I have signed a will that names him my heir. It is
stored with my accounts in your father's safekeep-
ing. Tell your son or tell him not as you wish. There
is just one thing I must add. One thing you must
know. If ever my son by some chance or act of the
gods is found alive then he not Mordec will inherit
all. Lovely and gracious lady I am ever your servant
Harald Goldmountain.'

Estrid did not hasten to send this news to Mordec
and Hauk (which was possible through Julius the
Troll who had his means of talking to people all over
the world). She pondered it. She knew there was
a chance Harald's son was still alive.

There was no sense, she thought, in saying, 'Expect
this to come to you but also expect it not to.'

She did not fear that Mordec would be angry or
bitter if he lost what was never his. She knew him
better than that. But a promise uncertain to be ful-
filled was not a real promise.

So Estrid counselled herself to keep it untold for
a time, and await events.

the maiden's song

Tove, mother of Gus, saw the bright side of Gus's disgrace. With all the other young men gone, she said to him more than once, the girls would be wanting his attention.

'But it's not something *I* want,' he said.

He soon found out how right his mother was. Girls smiled at him whenever they could catch his eye. If two or more together found themselves near him, they giggled and blushed.

One came often to visit his mother when he was home, but no sooner did she walk in than he thought of some excuse to hurry out.

There was a song heard everywhere, day and night. It came through the windows of houses and the open doors of workshops. It was even sung by old men drinking in the mead hall. It was a catchy little song.

He's gone to war,
I'll spin no more,
Forsake the pot and ladle.
Tell me now what beauty's for?
What is the use of the cradle?
Day into night, night into day,
The flowers of the morning are fading away.

'It's silly,' he said to Tove. 'The boys have only been gone a few days.'

But to his annoyance the tune stuck in his head, and he found himself humming it, even singing the words, as he went about doing what he needed to do to carry out his plan.

He had formed his plan long before the army had sailed.

First, he let himself be seen on the roads and in the shipyard. He went to the mead hall so that Mordec's mother would know he had not gone away.

Then one day he looked in at the armourer where Hengist-turned-Daedalus had worked. There he found Horsa's lame uncle, Aric. He had little to do but sharpen knives for the women and repair their pots and pans.

'Good morning,' Gus said cheerfully.

'Good morning to you,' the old man said.

'The army is lucky to have Daedalus with it. He'll come up with some fine ideas for weapons.'

'It's a good chance for him to test his weapons in a real war,' the old man said.

'He must have taken a lot of things with him,' Gus said. 'This place is much emptier than it was.'

'He was late getting to his ship,' Aric said. 'He was searching for something. A special suit of armour that he'd taken much trouble with.'

'The armour he was painting green and brown?' Gus asked.

'You saw it?'

'Yes. I remember asking him about it. I couldn't understand what his idea was, doing that. He stored it here, I remember.'

Gus went to a large chest and raised the lid.

'Gone,' he said.

'It's a mystery what happened to it.'

'A mystery,' Gus echoed, shaking his head at the strangeness of the thing.

Next he went to the warehouse of Bjarwulf the Pirate at Lovehaven, a nearby, small, secluded cove.

There he found, not Bjarwulf, but his accountant Pelf, bringing spears, bows, quivers, arrows, swords, daggers and battleaxes down from the shelves, placing them in rows on the floor, then going to his table to write something down.

It was as Gus expected. Bjarwulf, the only man left behind who was not old or crippled—or barred as Gus himself was by law from joining the army—was getting ready to sail. He was a man apart. The greatest pirate of them all. He was not expected to fight on land, but to terrorize the enemy at sea.

Pelf did not return his greeting. He was too busy. His lips moved as he went from the lines of weapons to his table, repeating the numbers. When Gus asked for the second time where he might find Bjarwulf, he looked at Gus for a moment or two, frowning, and finally replied, 'on the ship seven, nine, two.'

So to Bjarwulf's ship Gus was about to go, when Pelf's wife Delfinola came in.

'Gus son of Hakon!' she exclaimed. She swept back her long white hair and held up her arms as if in delighted surprise. 'Well, talk of the devil, as they say in Ireland—no offence intended. Wouldn't it be a joy for me now if you were to bide a while? I have some enchanting thoughts concerning you and a certain pretty maiden who has spoken of you to me in wistful words.'

'I—I have something—urgent—you see—that I have to—I must find Bjarwulf,' he stammered, sidling towards the door.

Delfinola put an arm about his shoulders. She was as tall as he.

'Dear friend to be held ever close,' she said, tightening her grip on his upper arm. 'I ask you to believe me when I say I know what is in your heart, and you would do well to speak of it with me rather than with himself, the powerful man.'

The pressure of her arm, the earnestness of her tone, the intense look in her eyes, and a stirring of curiosity brought him to a seat beside her on a bench some distance from Pelf's table, while Pelf himself carried on with his work, too absorbed in it to pay any attention to what the two of them were talking about.

'It is a sharp fate to be idle when all others are doing great deeds—I know it, how I know it,' she deeply sighed. 'Have I myself not wept standing by while heroes charged past me in chariots, and the cries of lost lovers died in the woods with the waning of the moon?'

Gus understood that she was expressing sympathy for his being left out of the army and the war. She surely had more to say than that!

She took one of his hands in both of hers, sighed again, and went on:

'Uncanny it would sound in a stranger's ears, as it did mine when first I was told, that a man who lives by plunder is strict for the law. But to a Viking born it cannot seem strange. It is the right way. It is the Viking way. Ever faithful to their own law, ever faithful to each other, they spare no enemy, his all is yours. You would ask Bjarwulf if you could sail with him.'

Gus felt his face grow hot, That was exactly what he'd planned to do.

'You would tell yourself, he is not part of the army. He is a lone wolf on the seas. If I sail with him and fight with him, neither he nor I will be breaking the law. Perhaps you even dreamt of leaving his ship if he came close perchance to England's shore, to seek a way there to aid the Viking warriors, may glory be theirs. And certain you would be that it was noble to do so. But he will say no. Believe me, dear friend who would act only honourably and nobly, he will say no. And he will blame you for asking, he will. So do not ask. And I will forever cherish what I have learnt from you, that you wished to act nobly. I will think of you always as one with a noble heart. Yes, today you have made me proud to know you, Gus son of Hakon. Go now, but go not where the Serpent of the Seas lies in its own harbour. Go not near Bjarwulf with that question on your tongue. Keep yourself apart, I say, though as I have told you I too have known how bitter loneliness can be.'

She rose, still holding his hand and drawing him to his feet. She let him go, and pointed to the door. 'My thoughts and esteem go with you, dear friend,' she said.

He left without saying a word. She had not asked him to *promise* that he would not ask Bjarwulf to let him sail on the Serpent of the Seas against the enemy.

As he walked away, thinking what he might do if that part of his plan had to be abandoned—and 'how did she know?' he kept wondering—he heard her voice, strong and musical, coming through the open door behind his back, singing the haunting words:

He's gone to war,
I'll spin no more,
Forsake the pot and ladle.
Tell me now what beauty's for?
What is the use of the cradle?
Day into night, night into day,
The flowers of the morning are fading away.

He knew she was not aiming the song at him. No taunt was intended. She sang often. She was a composer of songs. He should have guessed, he told himself, where that song had been born.

The general opinion was that Delfinola was better at composing poems and songs than the Skald, who 'might once have been a true poet, but had lost the fire from the gods since he started drinking too much', Gus's father had said, who was no light drinker himself.

He would take her advice and warning. But if he couldn't go with Bjarwulf, what other way might he find?

His thoughts were on England, and he recalled what had happened the first time he had been there. He had helped save Mordec from execution. He and Lily. His thoughts dwelt on Lily. He daydreamt that he was fighting her; and then that hewas marrying her. Which was it to be?

All this so occupied him as he walked slowly with his head down, hardly seeing where he was going, not even hearing the giggles of some girls who passed him on the road, that it was some time before the memory of the voyage itself, that time, to England and home again, stopped him as suddenly as if he had come up against a wall.

'Of course!' he said aloud. 'Of course. But where is it?'

Now he hurried. He ran through the shipyard among the half-built ships, the damaged ships, the broken ships, along the quays where fishing craft were tied, not pausing until he came to a small back-water under the overhang of the headland, and there he saw what he was looking for.

'Foal of the Foam,' he said aloud. And he laughed. 'Mordec's half-ship. It carried me to England once, it will carry me again.'

Was it seaworthy?

He found it was.

He packed it with all he'd need to take with him very late in the pale grey evening when few were about to see him running with burdens on his back.

He rowed away at midnight. It did not trouble him that he had no crew. He knew, he felt, that he could sail this little ship, this boys' craft, this well-made toy, alone as far as England.

When he was well away from the shore he raised the sail he had taken from one of the big ships and cut to size—a task that had taken feverish hours in the half-dark of a half-ruined shed. It fitted the mast. The morning breeze swelled it and Foal of the Foam gathered speed.

This was to be the little ship's last voyage. Once Gus had landed on the English shore it would be taken away forever by the tide. But now it drifted on the water smoothly as a swan.

Gus leant against the mast, easy at last, and found himself singing.

He's gone to war …

the charming smew

'Surely we fear the Vikings more than the Army of the Redeemed?' Father Donlock said to the Earl as they sat together in the counting-house the day after the battle of the Nijn.

'If I believed Abbot Alonso to be as good a man as you, Donlock, I would fear nothing from the Christian army. But we have heard how Botham Cogg has had to flee to Cornwall for shelter, ceding Felldown to the Abbot and his men if they choose to take it, and without an arrow being shot. Bummy Cogg is as Christian as I am, yet the Abbot threatened him and his entire earldom. He—or his plucky daughter—thought it prudent to take notice of what the Abbot's men did at the Castle of Yggdrasil. Not a soul spared, Donlock, not one.'

Father Donlock shook his head. 'Deplorable,' he said. 'Alonso de Llama is not what I understand a Christian to be.'

'And he is in command of the whole campaign,' Earl Reginald reminded the priest.

While the dreadful din of war had raged, the Earl and the people of Linkard had waited fearfully for the fighting to spill over into the earldom.

Father Donlock had suggested that if he, attired in his church vestments of cassock, surplice, chasuble and stole, stationed himself prominently within sight of the armies, perhaps holding up a shield with a cross on it, the Army of the Redeemed would see no need to enter the territory, correctly assuming it to be Christian country.

Princess Jessica had pointed out the danger, not just to him but to them all.

'Not all the Viking warriors know us, or know about our treaty with our Viking neighbours,' she said. 'They might see you simply as the enemy. A provocation, daring them to come in and conquer us.'

'That's all too possible,' the Earl had said in support of her view. 'Good of you though, Donlock. Brave. Honourable. I thank you for your loyalty to us.'

'I am a Linkardian born and bred,' Father Donlock had said. 'This land is my land.'

Now the Earl was in solemn mood, facing a perilous future.

'We were lucky,' he said. 'They let us be. But the trouble is far from over. Queen Bertha is coming to confer with us. She is bringing Anwid Cogg, Felldown's daughter with her. They will be here any moment now. We need to talk about gathering a strong defence force. You will join us, please, Donlock. We need all sober heads thinking about what's best to do. The future of England depends on it.'

Queen Bertha of the Fenreach (dressed in an amber-coloured robe with a cloak the colour of dark plums), her White Knight the Ethiope, Sir Baz (dressed all in white), her grand-daughter Queen Lily (dressed in her everyday boys' clothes), and Captain Anwid (dressed in the clothes she wore to go to sea), were at that moment approaching the castle, the four of them on two grand horses. The two queens were mounted on their splendid black stallion Maelstrom, Bertha sitting sideways behind Lily, who rode like a man. The Captain rode behind Sir Baz, astraddle his strong white gelding.

Because the meeting was to be an affair of state, a certain formality was observed. A groom waited in the forecourt to take care of the horses, and an officer of the guard with a yellow feather in his helmet led them ceremoniously over the drawbridge, through the castle, and down a colonnade to the counting-house.

The Earl embraced Queen Bertha, as always, with true affection. When all the courtesies of greeting were over and everyone was seated, the Earl opened the discussion by solemnly announcing, 'This is a council of war'.'

The talk was not cheerful. The question they all sought an answer to was, how many fighters could they muster to defend England?

They had lived with the Viking presence for years, but reckoned that now the Vikings' right to be there was being challenged by the Church, they would not be content with defending their settlements. They would fight to conquer more territory.

Old agreements and treaties could not be depended on.

And furthermore, the engagements between the Vikings and the Church's army would spread any-where, everywhere, over the land.

All agreed that an English defence force was urgently needed. But word had been brought to the earl that the powerful King of Mercia was not prepared to intercept the Army of the Redeemed, and would let them pass northward through his land to attack the Vikings on the border of Northumbria.

'The chances they will see us as easy conquests, and our fields as a clear passage through to the Viking thorp on our border, are all too likely,' said the Earl.

'They must think Vikings are still there,' Queen Bertha said. 'But Sir Baz informs me they have gone to join their army in the north.'

'Leaving a few old men behind for no reason I can think of,' Sir Baz said, in a tone that deplored the unreason of it.

The Earl said he had two hundred men under arms. Queen Bertha said she had a rabble of bumpkins full of zeal who would be willing to die for her and for England, but could not be relied on to kill for them try as they would.

'Sir Baz,' she added, 'is the greatest fighter in the world in single combat, but he cannot do the work of a regiment.'

'Not the work of a regiment,' Sir Baz agreed, 'though I warrant I'd lay out a fair number of them.'

'Sir Baz and I together,' Queen Lily said, 'could kill a hundred of them, whoever they are.'

She and Sir Baz nodded at each other, firm determination in their eyes.

'I have twenty girls,' Captain Anwid said. 'All trained and skilful fighters. And at my urgent request, King Mark of Cornwall has promised a thousand men. Also, he has called for an armed band from Wales, another few hundred.'

They sat in gloomy silence. 'About twelve hundred against an army of furious Vikings and perhaps also—perhaps even at the same time—an army of Christian devils. No offence intended, Father,' Anwid said.

'None taken,' Father Donlock assured her.

The same thought was in the minds of all. 'We will fight, but we will lose.'

The Earl began to ask, 'Is there anyone else we can turn to—', when he was interrupted by a servant.

'Someone has arrived to see you, my lord. He is armed, but the guards have not arrested him because he says he comes from the King of Mercia.'

'Ask him please to step in.'

A slender young man with long fair curly hair, wearing a short sky-blue tunic, a silver-link belt with a jewelled sword hanging from it, and blue sandals—their straps crisscrossed up his legs as far as the knees—entered, bowed elaborately, and introduced himself.

'Crispin Cuthburd, come to speak with Earl Reginald of Linkard for King Aelfrid of Mercia,' he said in a sing-song voice, and pronouncing Reginald as if it started with a W.

The Earl bent his head. Father Donlock and Sir Baz rose and bowed.

'Is there bad news?' the Earl asked.

'My Woyal Master has charged me to present a proposal concerning the defence of England that he trusts will be as congenial to Linkard as to Mercia.'

Upon which, Master Cuthburd was instantly invited to join the council, to each of whose members he was formally introduced.

King Aelfrid, he told them, had changed his mind about letting the Church Army pass unmolested through his land. He had an army ten thousand strong. It was his intention to defend his kingdom from the Pope's invasion. He proposed a military alliance of Merica and Linkard.

The proposal was instantly accepted: by the Earl and Jessica with relief; by Father Donlock and Sir Baz with gratitude mixed with unease; by Queen Bertha, Queen Lily, and Captain Anwid, with fiery delight.

'Splendid!' Bertha exclaimed.

'Yesss!' shouted Lily.

She and Anwid looked at each other and laughed with glee. Their smiles lingered, their eyes blazed. They were ready for battle.

'My King does not want war,' Crispin Cuthburd felt it necessary to explain, 'But he thinks it is inevitable. He is widely esteemed as a man of peace. We are not a violent nation. I regard myself as a typical Mercian, and I am against violence.' He looked at Sir Baz as he said this. 'I don't understand why we can't all just get along.'

Queen Bertha stopped smiling and fixed a look of scornful distaste on the young man, which, if he saw, he blandly ignored.

'The combined strength of Linkard, the Fenreach, Cornwall and Wales could be a little over six thousand men,' the Earl told the envoy. 'Six to seven thousand men of sterling quality ready to fight alongside the forces of Mercia.'

'My Royal Master will be delighted to hear it,' Crispin Cuthburd said, smiling. (Jessica though that the smile might be better described as a smirk, but she pushed the thought away as being uncharitable.)

The Earl asked Master Cuthburd to inform the King of their acceptance of his proposal.

'That I shall do,' the envoy said. 'But I have not yet delivered the full message with which I have been entrusted.'

'Well get on with it man!' exclaimed Queen Bertha.

'The King requests—and I must remind you, my lord and ladies, that a King's request is a command—that you send your forces, as soon as you can, for time is short, my lord and ladies, for time is short, as soon as you can, today if you can, not later than tomorrow, your forces, to join the Kings' army at Tamworth.'

The faces of his listeners fell. There was a moment's silence.

'He wants *our* forces to go and join *his* forces at Tamworth?' the Earl asked slowly.

'That is his request, or need I say his command, my lord.'

'King Aelfrid of Mercia,' said the Earl, 'is not my king. I do not obey commands, I give them. Now. First, the army from Cornwall has not yet arrived. Second, if I send our entire force to Tamworth, my land will have none to guard it. I have a treaty with the Vikings on our border, but it may not hold in a time of war. It would be more useful if King Aelfrid were to send reinforcements to us.'

'Your weply is that you decline to do as the King asks?'

'That is my reply. I am encouraged to hear that the King intends to engage the Church's invading army, and would welcome reinforcements, but I can spare no soldiers.'

Cuthburd rose, bowed his ornate bow and hurried to the forecourt, where a message-bearer, so eager to start back to West Mercia that he had not even dismounted from his racing mare, listened to Cuthburd, gabbled the words back to him to make sure he had the message right, and galloped away.

Cuthburd, returned to his hosts, bowed over Jessica's hand, and asked if he might stay awhile 'in this pleasant spot' so that 'the alliance may become all the stronger through friendship'.

Jessica looked at the Earl, who nodded, so she said in a tone of courtly formality, 'It would be an honour, Master Cuthburd.'

'We are glad to hear that in your view the alliance has been agreed on both sides, despite our disagreement over where our forces should be deployed,' said the Earl.

Later when he and Jessica and the Earl's art director, Mel de Gustybuss, were sitting in a courtyard where a fountain played, the envoy said, 'Please call me Crispin.'

And he went on, 'I must tell you gentle people, so that you know everything about me of importance, that as well as a courtier of the King's court, I am a poet.'

'A poet,' Jessica said politely.

'A poet!' Mel exclaimed delightedly. 'We haven't had a poet here before. Tell me, what costume do you wear when you recite your poems at court?'

'Oh, no special clothes,' Crispin admitted.

'I'll design something for you, if you'll allow me.' Mel said. 'Love to! I like the colour you're wearing, but I'd have something more flowing. Not necessarily longer—it would be a shame to cover those classic sandals, straight from Mercury I thought as soon as I saw them—but loose from the shoulders, light enough to blow back. Pleated, perhaps.'

'That would be really good of you.'

Jessica noticed that not all his Rs were spoken as Ws. It wasn't a lisp, it was a performance.

By early evening the pleated cape in sky-blue was ready for Crispin to wear. Mel found him dozing on a bench alone in the courtyard where the fountain played and took him to his workshop. Peering over his eyeglasses, Mel put in some pins where a few extra stitches were needed too make the short cape fit better on the shoulders.

'Princess Jessica is very beautiful,' Crispin said. 'Is she betrothed?'

'M-m,' Mel replied without opening his mouth, having pins clasped between his lips.

'No? She must have many admirers.'

'Now the other shoulder,' Mel said when his mouth was free. 'I can't tell you how great a pleasure it is to dress someone who cares about his appearance.'

'I make my own designs usually,' Crispin said. 'The King doesn't think much of them, but the Queen likes them. Or so she says. She also likes my poetry. Or so she says.'

He gazed thoughtfully out of the window.

'I see you have a lake, Mel,' he said.

'We have five lakes in Linkard, Crispin. That one's called Royston Thump.'

'Thump? Why thump? Does it have some monster living in it who thumps its scaly tale?'

'No, thump is an old word for a lake hereabouts.'

'It inspires me to a poem,' Crispin said. 'I shall st-woll that way and see if the Muse fancies me today.'

'You might find the air less than pleasant over there,' Mel said. 'An unwholesome odour is wafting from the riverbanks where there was a battle two days ago. Many were slain. The bad smell seems to linger in the low ground.'

The poet waved away the objection. He went boldly running, fleet of foot, over the meadows to the lake. Mel watched him go, pleased to see that the light cape, as he had hoped, fluttered behind him as he ran. (But Crispin found the smell really was bad, and he did not stay long by the lake.)

Meanwhile Jessica and Father Donlock were working with the Earl on a letter to King Aelfrid. They all had thoughts and questions about where soldiers of the English army should be placed.

'Might a part of it be stationed on the western border of the Fenreach,' the Earl enquired.

'Where were the armies most likely to face each other next,' Jessica wondered.

'Should I offer to act as a peacemaker between the English and the Church?' Father Donlock asked.

When the letter was finished, signed, sealed and taken by Father Donlock to a messenger to deliver it with all speed to King Aelfrid, the Earl and his daughter stood together at the window of the counting-house, looking at their green fields, dark woods, and lakes that they knew teemed with many-coloured fish.

'Better to enjoy the outdoors from indoors today,' the Earl said. 'At least the smell of the rotting corpses hasn't penetrated into the castle. Or not yet, but—look—there by the lake—the Cuthburd fellow.'

'I see him,' Jessica said.

'A good-looking young man,' the Earl said. 'And a poet, you tell me? I understand it's the fashion for high-born young ladies to fall in love with handsome young poets who have neither rank nor fortune. If that should happen to you, my dear, you won't find me the sort of tyrannical father who forbids such an attachment.'

'Father,' Jessica said, 'When I marry, it will be to a man of rank and fortune, land and title,'

'Sensible girl' the Earl said.

The next day, when the two queens, Sir Baz, Captain Anwid and the Mercian visitor were dining in the great hall of Linkard Castle, Master Cuthburd offered to recite a poem he had composed. Without waiting for anyone's assent, he rose and began:

On Woyston Thump
The charming Smew
Slackens the caring
Hunter's thew.

He looked round the table for praise.

'Very … original,' said the Earl. 'What do you think, Jessica my dear?'

The poet smiled at Jessica.

'I hope *you* like it, Lady Jessica,' he said.

'I don't quite understand it,' Jessica said gently, not wanting to hurt his feelings.

The poet's smile became less assured.

'What's it mean?' Lily demanded gruffly.

The poet sat down and patiently explained. 'Woyston Thump, as you no doubt all know, is your lake. On the lake there swims a kind of duck called a Smew. I have heard of Smews. I saw a picture of one, and it seems to be forever smiling. I found that charming. I don't know if any of the ducks on the lake were Smews, so I was just using my poetic imagination. I imagine myself to be a hunter who is so charmed by the face of the Smew that I cannot bring myself to kill it, though I raise my bow and ready the arrow. I drop my arms again, let my muscles relax, rather than shoot that duck once it has turned its smile and its round innocent eyes on me.'

'Obscure,' said Father Donlock.

'But pretty?' Mel de Gustybuss suggested out of pity for the poet.

Queen Bertha leant towards the Earl's ear and confided to him loudly, '"*The charming Smew?*", "*The caring hunter's thew?*" I'd have a man savaged by beasts for writing stuff like that. If he's typical of Aelfrid's men, having ten thousand of them mincing about a battlefield will do *nothing* to save England.'

plot and counter-plot

When Abbot Alonso heard of the defeat of his invading forces in the battle of the Nijn, his Black Monks expected him to erupt in fury. They waited, stiff and afraid, as the messengers stood before him in his office and gave him the news, blow after blow.

'A rout, a rout, a veritable rout!'

'Huge losses … few survivors …'

'Mile after mile, on every piece of solid ground in the marshy delta, all the way up the banks of the Nijn to the border of Linkard, there they were—Christian bodies fixed on poles, their hearts exposed to the birds, their ribs spread out like white and crimson wings …'

The Abbot listened in silence. They finished, and still he said nothing. He rose and went without uttering a word to the abbey church. His usual attendants followed him, but he stopped them at the door, went in alone and shut them out.

They looked through the windows. One among them who did not really belong with them was to report a long time afterwards to Sam of the West: 'He stood there. Just stood. He didn't kneel the way Christians do in a church. He stood still without saying anything. All the time he was looking up at the picture of the god nailed on a cross, not as if he was asking for something, not as if he wanted to be comforted or forgiven or anything like that. I mean, he had sent all those men to their deaths and he's supposed to be a Christian so he might have felt sorry for them. Christians spend a lot of time feeling sorry for people. They pray for their souls, but I'm sure he wasn't praying. He was glaring up at the god. Like this—as if he was scolding him.'

Revenge was brewing in Alonso's heart.

That much Sam could guess. For that he did not need to hear talk of it through the tubes that Alonso had put in the wall between them. But it had been a cause for regret that he could no longer learn any-thing that way. Alonso had blocked the tubes when he realized that the tower could listen to his abbey through them just as his abbey could listen to the tower.

Then something began to happen that made up for Sam's loss of the tubes. He received messages, slipped into laundry baskets or baker's trays or ped-dler's bundles by an informer who never wrote his name on them.

From this unknown source he learnt that eleven thousand Christian soldiers had started from their camping grounds round Yggdrasil Castle, and were now waiting south of London to be joined by another thousand stationed on the border of Felldown. They would proceed north-west to into the Kingdom of Mercia, storm the palace at Tamworth, and demand the King's submission to the authority of the Pope.

Sam would not have been easily and immediately persuaded that what the unknown source told him was true. It could have been a trick by his enemy the Abbot to mislead him. But there was a sign that the writer was a friend. The letters were formed exactly the way Djil formed them. Djil formed them in a way no one else did. And that could only mean one thing: that she had taught the nameless person how to write. She had taught none of the Black Monks. Even if she had been willing to, which she was not, they had no need of her teaching; they could all read and write. She had taught only a few persons, all of whom she had judged to be friends. So Sam believed his informer.

He talked to his grandmother about Alonso's intended invasion of England. 'He's been thoroughly beaten by the Vikings, and he must be planning his revenge on them. But first, it seems, he means to subdue the English themselves. His long held ambition to rule all the islands of the west has not changed.'

He asked for her opinion. Should he or should he not interfere in the war? By reputation he was so wise as to be infallible, but the truth was that he himself never stopped questioning his own understanding. A talk with his grandmother often helped him to see more clearly; not because she always had good advice for him, but because by expressing his thoughts he could make them clearer to himself.

He told her he suspected that while Alonso's spoken aim was to convert the whole of England and all the Western Isles to Christianity, his unspoken ambition was to be the Pope's representative there. Not just his ambassador—his 'nuncio'—but his viceroy; to govern in his name with unlimited power.

The Abbot had considerable influence over the present Pope, who was weak in body and weaker in mind.

'The Pope will appoint him nuncio,' Sam said, 'and he will rule like a monarch. His word will be law. And he won't use his power well.'

'He's a tyrant born,' Djil agreed.

'What I ask myself,' Sam said, 'is whether I should do anything to impede his plans.'

'Alonso must be stopped,' Djil said, voicing Sam's own unspoken thought.

So Sam was considering how to get a message to King Aelfrid of Mercia, when another message came that Alonso had changed his plans. It was a short note plucked from the ear of a freshly delivered pig's head and brought to him from the kitchen. It said that Alonso's men would now march north along the margin of the wild forest of east Mercia, but instead of turning west to reach Tamworth, they would turn east to take the weakly defended Earldom of Linkard, and from there mount an overwhelming surprise attack on the Vikings in their settlement beside the Earldom.

'He wants his revenge first, after all!' Sam said. 'He's going after the Vikings again. And he'll happily destroy a small English earldom to get at them.'

About that there was something Sam could do at once. He could get a timely warning to Linkard. It must fly, and fly it would. For Sam's messengers had wings. They were feathered all in grey, or fawn, or speckled white. Sam called them his 'doves'. Julius the Troll had sent them to him with trusted traders early in the summer. They carried letters on their legs to their home however many miles away in the North.

Julius would send the letters on to the Earldom of Linkard. Sam knew who would receive them there: the Art Director to the Earl, another correspondent of Julius, to whom also he had recently sent a crate of the birds. Sam knew this because Mel de Gustybuss—the Art Director—had sent him letters through the Troll asking him for drawings of the clothes the lords and ladies of southern France were wearing this year. His grandmother had made the sketches, coloured them beautifully, even adding touches of gold leaf, cut them up into small squares and helped him dispatch them to the north on pigeons' legs.

'What will the Earl of Linkard do when he hears that at any moment the Pope's army of conquest will descend on his land?' Sam asked himself and his grandmother.

'Ask King Aelfrid for help?' Djil suggested.

'Most likely,' Sam said. 'But even if King Aelfrid decides to send a legion or two, they would take time to get there. So wouldn't the Earl of Linkard warn his neighbours the Vikings and make common cause with them? The English get along well enough with them most of the time. In some ways they'd be better off without them because they're dedicated pillagers. But their presence has kept out far worse invaders and settlers. The battle of the Nijn should have proved to the English that they need the Vikings on their side against the Army of the Redeemed. I believe this message will force an alliance between the English and the Vikings. I will say so.'

Sam sent the warning and the advice. How it was acted on was not for him to decide.

What neither he nor the Abbot knew was that there were no Vikings on the border of Linkard, except a few old men left behind to guard their property from neighbourhood thieves.

a royal command

Commander Tostig brought the force that had won the battle of the Nijn to the fields round his headquarters at Barleyfield Monastery.

'The main body of Alonso's hordes,' Tostig said, bending over a map drawn by Mordec, the chain mail that he never took off in his waking hours clinking as he did so, 'are moving over land. Some two thousand have started northward from his southern headquarters at Yggdrasil Castle down here. They will join a greater force of about seven thousand at present camping here, on the border of the Earldom of Felldown. I have a reliable report that they are planning to attack us in our deserted settlement here, on the River Nijn, the region we have just so sweetly rid of them. My guess is they will move west, then north through Mercia along the edge of the forest, then east through the Fenreach and the Earldom of Linkard. He would lay them waste as he goes. But he may prefer to proceed north-east from the River Tamesis through this region here. What sort of territory is it, Mordec?'

'It's wilderness in the lower region,' Mordec replied. 'Nearer to our settlement there are scattered villages. The entire region west and south of the

Fenreach is nominally under the rule of King Aelfrid of West Mercia, but our raids on the villages have discouraged him from interfering, so each village is really just a small independency. We let them farm and breed horses, and they let us take what we want when we want it, rather than risk losing everything. It's worked well like that for a long time now. I'm sure they would just let the Christian army pass through if it came up that way. They wouldn't fight for themselves, let alone for us. But—may I ask you something, Commander?'

'Ask,' Tostig said. He suspected that whatever the young mapmaker had to say might be worth hearing.

'Although we can trust that the report was true when it was sent, what if by now Alonso has learnt that we have moved the whole army up here? He will continue his march due north to meet us here, below or above Barleyfield Ridge. Of course we would make sure he does not come up over the ridge. We would descend on his forces.'

'Hmm. Hmm. I think I would have heard if he had changed his plans.'

'But we will be ready for him on the Ridge anyway, won't we?' Mordec asked.

Tostig was still looking closely at the map. 'He might split his forces—send some this way to try us again here, and the rest press on to attack us up here.'

'Yes,' Mordec said. 'I see that's what he might do.'

'What is the ground like, just south of Barleyfield Ridge? Is it marshy? Are there homesteads? Boulders?'

'I don't know,' Mordec said. 'I need to find out.'

'*Now*,' the Commander ordered. 'Go. I need to know *now*.'

Mordec set out at once. He had to weigh speed against accuracy. If he rode over the ground he had to inspect he would miss much. But if he walked, he would be slow, when the Commander was in a hurry to know what he would find. Having to choose between accuracy and speed, he chose accuracy.

He and Leif rode westward to Barleyfield Ridge. There he dismounted and handed the reins of his horse to Leif.

'Meet me back here with my horse when the sun starts to go down. That's when your shadow starts to be longer than you are.'

'I should be coming with you to look after you,' Leif said sternly. 'What if you lost your glasses?'

'I won't lose my glasses,' Mordec said. 'They'll be on my nose when I see you again. No harm will come to me. If I meet the Army of the Redeemed, I'll just turn round and come back.'

Leif decided he would stay where he was to wait for Mordec. He found a shady tree, sat with his back against it, and let the horses graze.

In the distance in one direction were the tents of the Viking soldiers; in the other, training grounds where soldiers were being drilled.

Men in armour on horseback or on foot came by every few minutes. Some of them stopped to talk to him, although he didn't know them. They asked him was he an English boy or had come with the army. 'I'm a Viking,' he replied, and they would smile at the pride in his voice, and move on.

Mordec did not know that four riders were following him. Their orders were to keep him in sight.

'Don't wear armour. Stay at a distance. Only go to his aid if necessary,' Tostig had told them. 'He must not know you are following him.'

Mordec's protection was not the Commander's only reason for sending the men after his mapmaker. He was making sure that the report he needed came back to him. It would be a sad and even a serious loss if Mordec did not return, but a failure to inflict a decisive defeat on the Army of the Redeemed through not knowing the lie of the land would be disastrous.

'While you are down there,' he told the men, 'look carefully at the ground. When you return I may want you to tell me where it is stony or wet. Look out for any houses, farms, farmers, herds, streams. Be ready to make a full report.'

Mordec, looking like any English traveller, without armour, but with his sword at his side, began his descent to the plain, which was flat and green as far as he could see to the south and the west. There were no houses. On the east there was forest, ideal cover for an ambush, so perhaps good news for the Commander.

It was an easy descent. When he reached the bottom, he took off his glasses, polished them with the hem of his tunic, replaced them, and started briskly due south. 'It can't all be like this,' he reasoned, 'or it would be farmed. I'll come to stony ground soon, I'd bet on it.'

He had not gone far when he heard the rhythmic beating of drums coming from the west. He paused to see who or what was approaching. Slowly they became visible to him. Men marching to the drumbeat … one in front leading them in shining boots … two drummers one on each side of the front line of four … line after line in step behind them … and … a flag. Someone in the third or fourth line was carrying a yellow flag with a large black O on it.

'The flag of Owaindale!'

He had to think quickly. Why were they here? Where were they going?

The only likely destination was Linkard. The Earl must be gathering allied forces. This gallant little force from the happy Princedom of Owaindale were too few to be much help to the English cause, and were all too likely to be destroyed in the coming battles.

He felt sad for them as if they really were his own people.

And there was another reason to stop them.

They could not be long in the region of Linkard and the Fenreach without learning who their wandering Prince, the Prince they loved and trusted, really was.

He felt, as before, shame for deceiving them, but knew he would feel worse—guilt, dishonour—if he broke his promise to the Princess Angharad to preserve the myth by which she consoled her people and received their loyalty; the myth that their Prince was alive and merely absent on his travels.

'What to do? What to do?'

A moment more and he knew what to do. He ran towards them, smiling, stretching out both his arms as if to gather them all to his heart.

'Well met, my people,' he called as soon as they could hear him. 'Well met, well met.'

The leader stopped, and put up a hand to signal the company to halt.

The drums fell silent.

The leader peered through the eye-holes of a leather helmet that covered the rest of his face, saw who it was greeting them … saw the eyeglasses … He flung off his helmet, took two strides forward, and dropped on his knees.

'Your Highness!' he shouted with delight.

Mordec knew him. He was the hunter who had become his friend in the country he had ruled for a short and happy time as Prince Madoc.

'Fletch!' he shouted.

He touched the hunter's shoulder, asked him to rise, and the two men embraced each other.

Fletch turned to face his men.

'It is our Prince,' he shouted. 'Prince Madoc is here!'

A cheer went up. Smiles appeared on all the faces Mordec could see.

'He will now lead us,' Fletch shouted.

Another cheer went up.

Mordec, seeing what must have happened, and wanting to sound as if he knew much more than he did, said, 'You have been marching for days …'

Fletch nodded. 'Up along the valley of the River Wye then east beside the Severn,' he said. 'Now we are on our way to help defend the Earldom of Linkard. The King of Cornwall called upon our Princess to

125

help oppose the Christian army coming to conquer England and Wales.'

'Is the King of Cornwall sending soldiers too?'

'The Princess said he is sending ten thousand.'

'I don't know how many of you my sister decided to send.'

'Two hundred.'

Mordec said, 'I came to meet you as soon as I could. I'm only just in time to stop you. To save you all! Just over the hill there is a large platoon of mounted Vikings. It is an ambush. The news of your coming somehow reached them. Luckily it reached me first. If you go forward, they will descend on you and it will be a massacre. We will fight valiantly, but few if any of us will survive.'

Fletch looked towards the hill, and sure enough there on the crest, dark against the sky, were four horsemen.

'Turn about,' Mordec ordered. 'Go back. Do not beat your drums, put away our flag, do not march, but move as fast as you can, all the way home. Don't wait, don't ask me anything more. Go and save yourselves. I can tell you this—the Christian army will be defeated, but the small forces of Linkard will suffer great losses. I cannot save them but I can save you. Go, Fletch my good friend, go!'

Obediently Fletch shouted to his men to retreat. 'Break ranks, move fast, don't stop till I tell you …'

'Farewell!' Mordec called. 'Tell my sister I came in time to save you.'

'Will you not come with us?' Fletch paused to plead.

'This is no time for me to return. I have urgent work to do. For us all. Run, Fletch, run …'

Brave though they were, the men of Owaindale obeyed their Prince and ran.*

Mordec had not thought of glancing towards the hill himself, so he was not aware that in the last few moments four mounted men had begun to descend the hill.

The four had watched him veer towards a company of marching men in full armour and carrying spears. They could even faintly hear drums. They waited and watched to see what the mapmaker might do next. They had been ordered to come to his aid if he fell into danger; they had been told what to do if he came to harm; they had not been told what to do if he ran towards a troop of soldiers and embraced their leader.

They looked at each other as if to ask: does anyone know what we ought to do? Thoughts raced through their minds. Should they return to the Commander for further orders? Or should they simply go and ask Mordec who the soldiers were and why he was so friendly with them—so breaking their orders by revealing their presence?

Then the same awful notion struck all of them. Was this treachery they were watching? *Treason*? Was Mordec the mapmaker in league with a foreign power, an opposing army?

They looked at each other again and nodded, each to all. They knocked their heels hard into the sides

---

* Scholars say there is little doubt it is because of this event that the people of Owaindale say, to this day, that in times of danger Prince Madoc will appear to save their nation.

of their steeds and rode down to the plain, shouting, 'Halt! Stay!'

They drew their swords.

Mordec turned his head to see what the shouting was about. Fletch heard it too, stopped and looked back. What he saw made him run all the faster, urging his men to do the same.

'The Vikings are after us, as our Prince said they would be.'

It did not occur to him to fear for the Prince himself, because Fletch believed, as all the folk of Owaindale believed, that he was protected by magic.

'Halt? Stay? Do they mean me?' Mordec wondered, turning slowly to face the men charging fiercely towards him.

Who were they?

He saw their swords flashing in the sunlight and his hand reached for his own weapon but stopped when the wholly unexpected happened: another man, riding a huge black horse, and wearing the strangest leather armour mottled green and grey and a helmet that hid his face, rode right up beside him, holding his left arm stiffly down, and yelled—though the voice was dulled and the words distorted by the metal of the helmet—'Grab hold, Mordec, mount, trust me, trust me!'

Mordec saw the only way to certain safety. He grabbed the arm, leapt, and was on the back of the moving horse behind the rider before he knew how he'd managed to get there.

The horse carried him and his rescuer eastward towards the shelter of the forest at a speed few horses could match.

The four Vikings reined in their mounts, waited a moment or two, gaping at the fleeing horse with its two riders, and only then turned their horses heads that way and urged them to a gallop in pursuit. But they saw the distance grow between themselves and their quarry. They saw the black horse plunge among the trees and disappear in the thick shade.

They had lost Mordec, and had failed to carry out their orders.

Still they rode at a careful walking pace into the forest. They shouted Mordec's name. 'We only want to talk to you!' they bawled. 'Mordec! Mordec!' No answer came.

They searched until the shafts of sunlight striking through the leaves to the forest floor faded with the passing of the day.

They came together to confer. What would the Commander expect them to do? Go on searching until they found him, for days if necessary? Or return for further orders?

Two said 'search', and two said 'return'. Then two changed their minds. They would all return to report what had happened.

They rode close together.

One said: 'Do you think we should go after the marching men? Find out who they are and what Mordec said to them?'

'We could catch them easily before it's really dark,' said another.

'I think we need orders to do that,' said a third.

'Let's take a vote,' said the fourth. 'Who's for going after the men?'

Only his own hand went up.

'Then unless you want to go alone we'll all go back for new orders.'

'Or be put in chains,' said the second.

'Or worse,' said the first.

'Best we stick together,' said the third.

They urged their horses up the slope of the Ridge, and they reached Barleyfield Monastery soon after dark.

Their unexpected report did not, to their relief, anger the Commander. It made him frown in puzzlement. He asked many questions, some more than once: 'Who were the soldiers?'; 'Where did this horseman come from?'; 'How could it be that no one saw him coming?'.

They could give no answers to help him solve any part of the puzzle.

Then the Commander thought of asking Leif to help him solve it. He put out the word that Leif was to be brought to him.

Leif waited on the Ridge with ever growing anxiety. From time to time he had stepped out into the sunshine and looked at his shadow. It had grown distinctly longer than he was, and Mordec had not returned. When a patrol of mounted guards told him the Commander wanted to see him, he protested.

'I can't come with you. I promised Mordec I'd wait for him.'

'The Commander wants to talk to you. Perhaps it's about Mordec. Come with us and you'll soon know.'

He knew he had no choice but to ride with them. One of them led Mordec's horse.

'Has something happened? Is it bad news? Has something happened to Mordec?' Leif asked several times. But they couldn't answer him.

'Did the commander look angry? Or sad? How did he look?'

'We didn't see him. We only know he asked for you. You'll soon have your answers.'

'But Mordec told me to wait for him.'

'He'll find the way without you.'

'But he'll think I forgot to come for him …'

Leif's heart was beating hard as he stepped through the door into the presence of the Commander.

'Come in, Leif. I have something to ask you.'

'To ask me? But—but—aren't you going to tell me where Mordec is?'

'At this moment I have no idea where Mordec is.'

The alarm on Leif's face prompted the Commander to add quickly. 'But I'm sure he'll be back soon.'

'How do you know?'

'You and I know Mordec, don't we? Come and sit here beside me. There are some things about Mordec that you know and I don't, and I want you to tell me what you know.'

The Commander related to the boy what the four men had reported to him.

'Now can you tell me anything that might explain what happened. What Mordec might have said to the strange soldiers marching with the flag.'

'They say it was a yellow flag with a big O on it?'

'That's what they say.'

Leif gave one of his long low whistles. 'Owaindale!' he said. 'We—he—ruled Owaindale, you see. Mordec was the Prince of Owaindale. Is. Is the Prince. That's why they turned back. He must have told them to go back. To run away. They would do anything he told them to do.'

Tostig was impatient at first with Leif telling in his own way the tale of their time in the little Welsh country of Owaindale, recalling among other details the royal meals he had eaten there. But soon the Commander found himself being entertained by the story, and at the end of it he understood why Mordec had turned the soldiers back: he was saving them from finding out who he really was.

Tostig also guessed correctly that they had been coming as reinforcements for the English against Alonso. Such a small force—'a few hundred at most', the men had reported—would not have made a significant difference to the war.

If they had more to tell of troop movements, Mordec would report it all to him when he returned.

Of that the Commander had no doubt. Mordec would return with even more to tell than he had hoped for.

The only complete mystery that still remained—and which Tostig said not a word about to the anxious child—was why he had gone off willingly with the strange knight on the big black horse.

in a clearing

The big black horse leapt over a thicket, both wide and high, carrying though it was the weight of two riders, one of them in heavy armour, with an ease that few others of its kind could equal.

'They won't get to us here.'

The speaker reined in his splendid steed.

He dismounted, and Mordec let himself drop to the ground on the other side.

They were in a clearing of the forest, with a stream running through it, sparkling in patches of sunlight.

'You can show your face now, Gus,' Mordec said as he went to scoop up water, first to drink and then to cool his head and neck.

'When did you …?'

'Know it was you? What other strange rider would know my name? Where did you get that weird armour?'

'Hengist—I mean Daedalus—made it for himself. I stole it.'

'Who were those men? D'you know?'

'No idea.'

'They could've been Vikings. They may have wanted to protect me.'

'Did you want to wait and find out? When they were rushing down on you with their swords drawn?

No, you didn't. You leapt up behind me. I didn't capture you, I saved you. You haven't thanked me yet.'

'I'll thank you when I know what you saved me from. Tell me—how did you know where I'd be? Have you been following me?'

'Yes. But I won't come near you when you're in battle. Only—

'Only what?'

'Only if you're wounded.'

'When I suggested that you might become a lone warrior like Sir Baz, I didn't mean you to become my guardian.'

There was a long silence between them. Then Mordec asked, 'How did you get to England?'

Gus made no reply. Something about his silence made Mordec turn his head to look at him. He saw amusement and uneasiness on Gus's face.

'You didn't, did you? By yourself? In Foal of the Foam?'

Gus looked away, but he still wore a faint smile.

Mordec said no more about it. He didn't even ask where the small ship was.

Gus came to the stream, drank, and then demanded to know: 'Who were the marching men you turned back? What was that flag?'

'You were watching all that time? You saw me ...? They were my other people. The ones I ruled over for a time.'

'So if those men riding at you with their swords waving were Vikings and they saw you embracing the leader of a foreign army ...'

'I can tell my Viking people the truth. It's my Owaindale people I have to lie to.'

'"My people", "my people". Listen to yourself. You think those shouting men would've listened to you before they cut you down or tied you up?'

'If they were Vikings they wouldn't have killed me. They'd have taken me back to Tostig and *he* would believe me. In fact, I've got to tell Tostig that King Aelfrid is gathering forces against the Christians. There are ten thousand coming from Cornwall. There will be a big battle. The Christians can't fight two enemies at once. If we come down on them from the north while they are fighting Aelfrid on the west … I must go now. I'll take that horse. He's fast. If those men come after me he can outrun them. I'll wager his name is Maelstrom. Right?'

Gus smiled widely. 'Right.'

'Did Lily let you have him, or did you take him?'

'I took him. I'll take him back to her—though he's mine really. He remembered me. Must have, or he wouldn't have let me ride him. He's the fastest horse in the world. But he won't let you ride him.'

'He will. He must. You and Lily can fight over him later. Or share him. It's a good reason for you to marry her.'

Mordec moved towards the horse. 'Tell her I've got Maelstrom and I'll return him when I can.'

Gus was right. Maelstrom would not let Mordec ride him. He moved away as Mordec approached, not once but several times. At this, Gus laughed.

'Told you so,' he said.

Gus put on his helmet, took the reins in his hands and mounted. Maelstrom stood still.

'He'll let you ride behind me again. Come on, get up.'

Mordec hesitated. 'You cannot take me all the way. You cannot come among the soldiers.'

'I'll leave you where I found you then.'

That would do. Once he'd climbed the Ridge, Mordec would find Vikings to get him to the monastery and Tostig. Or Leif might still be there with the horses. So the two riders returned through the forest and on to the foot of the Ridge.

'Take Maelstrom home to Lily,' Mordec said as he dismounted. 'And tell her …'

'What? What shall I tell Lily?' Gus called as Mordec was hurrying away.

'Tell her I love her madly and want to marry her,' Mordec called.

'Liar!' Gus roared after him.

king aelfrid almost devises his famous historical act

King Aelfrid of Mercia was a grand king, He was tall, his presence was commanding, he was famously handsome. His black hair hung straight over his ears to the base of his neck. His black moustache arched over his very red lips. His beard was black and pointed. His cheeks were as red as his lips. His eyes were so dark a brown as to seem black.

He was the first king in England whose ceremonial cloak of crimson silk was edged all round with ermine.

He wore his crown when he sat with his council every day between the hours of ten in the morning and three in the afternoon—with a break for luncheon between one and two—in the throne hall of his many-towered ivy-covered palace at Tamworth. It was a beautiful crown of delicate gold filigree, with precious jewels—a diamond, a ruby, an emerald, a sapphire and a pearl—decorating its five highest peaks.

His black-haired, red-lipped, red-cheeked wife, Queen Aethelwynn, matched him almost in height, almost in beauty, and wore a cloak edged almost all the way round with ermine, and a crown almost as richly jewelled when she sat beside him on a throne almost as large as his.

Their two sons, Aedwin and Aedward, were beautiful, but kept out of the throne hall and the public eye except on special occasions.

They were being schooled by the best teachers in the world. (Aedwin would one day father Uther, famous in history as the Pendragon, and through him become—though after his own death in battle—the grandfather of the even more famous King Arthur.)

The full complement of ten councillors sat in a semi-circle facing the thrones. They were all old white-haired men who had fought old wars and begotten sons and grandsons who would fight wars to come.

Two russet-liveried officers of the palace stood on one side, holding up a map of England, Cornwall, Wales, Northumbria and Scotland.

Clad in the blue leather of his military uniform, the Duke of Bassington, First Commander under the King of the Mercian army—a muscular, bald, clean-shaven giant, with a face that bore a strong resemblance to those of the bulldogs he bred—held a long gold-painted arrow fletched with the breast feathers of golden eagles, ready to point to the map as the King spoke of where armies would traverse the land and where battle would be engaged.

The King was speaking, and everyone else sat very still, listening, because grave matters of state were being considered.

'Alonso,' said the King quietly but impressively in his deep voice, 'the bitter abbot of low descent who craves power and has beguiled the Holy Father into giving it to him, is determined to conquer these islands. All of them. He told the Holy Father that his aim was to Christianize them and bring every inch of them under the sway of the Holy See. But I have had many a report of him, and all agree that it's not for the glory of Christ that he wants to subdue and command these islands, but for the glory and power of Alonso de Llama himself. Else why is he planning—and I know that he is planning—to take his Army of the Redeemed even into Ireland which is as fully Christianized as Rome itself? He expects the Pope, on his demand, to appoint him Nuncio to a united Britain. He would keep all the princes and earls of England, Scotland, Cornwall and Wales in uncertainty. He intends to be the real power over all the lands. A despot, who will tax us until we are eating crusts and are clothed in rags. "For the Church," he will say, but he will dine off our gold plate on the meat of our cattle. Do you doubt any part of what I have told you, Councillors?'

'Councillors?' echoed the Queen.

A murmur and a shaking of white heads answered the King and Queen.

'His first plan was to conquer us, the largest kingdom, and send his missionaries and armies out from here, from Tamworth. So our spies in France and Rome sent word in cipher to us with our traders. As you know, in preparation to defend our kingdom against such an assault, we did what we could to augment our military strength. We applied to the King of Cornwall for reinforcements, pointing out to him that Alonso's ambition included the conquest of his territory too.'

'His territory too,' the Queen said.

'And as you know, King Mark complied with my request and promised me ten thousand men.'

'Ten thousand men,' the Queen emphasized.

'He went further, and persuaded a Welsh independency, a small but prosperous princedom, to contribute a few hundred fighters, using the same persuasive argument we had used with him, that Alonso plans to bring every part of these islands under his sway. I began to feel confident that we would have the strength to fight off our attackers.'

'Fight off our attackers,' the Queen echoed.

'We also planned to gather able-bodied men from our own region to swell our ranks. I started by sending a request for reinforcements to Earl Reginald of Linkard and the Queens of the Fenreach. Thinking of the Queens, we sent—as you will be aware, Councillor Cuthburd, your son as our emissary. Among the ladies of our own court, he is a favourite.'

'A favourite,' the Queen confirmed.

'But the Queens and the Earl, as we reported to you, sent a less than satisfactory reply, saying that they could spare no soldiers because they had too few for their own defence and needed every one they had.

Councillor Cuthburd looked apologetic.

'Now at that stage nothing had been said about Alonso planning to attack *their* lands. Still, I not only accepted their refusal, I told them I understood their anxiety. I even asked King Mark to direct the Welsh contingent to Linkard. I hoped thereby to convince them of my good will and look for theirs in return.

And it seemed just as well that I did. We have heard, to our very great relief, that Alonso's plans have changed. He intends to pass us by, to leave us quite unmolested under certain conditions that I will come to. His aim, we learn, is first and before all else, to avenge his defeat by the Vikings in the battle of the Nijn. His will march his men through the Fenreach and Linkard and fall upon the Vikings in their settlement … Yes, there it is … Thank you, Bassington.'

The eyes of the Councillors followed the arrow as it moved over the map.

'The best advice we can give the Earl and the Queens—especially as the Welsh forces have not arrived—is not to resist. To give Alonso free passage through to the Vikings. Do you agree?'

'Agree?' asked the Queen.

The white heads nodded.

'Which brings me to the important proposal we need to put before you today. We ask you all please to consider it carefully. Advise us if we are reasoning poorly, or missing some vital factor we need to reckon with. As you know, it has long been our wish to unite all England under our rule. As we often remind others, ours is the largest kingdom. It is true that our writ does not run at present in the forests of the east where outlaws pursue their wild ways, preying on the thorps of the eastern marshlands, and the folk live lawless lives in fear between the pillaging Vikings and the robber bands. Why do we not enforce our rule over them? What stands in our way of bringing all England under our sway? We'll say it flatly: the Vikings. The Vikings stand in our way. They will not be ruled. They are a fierce people who live by piracy and plunder. Even when they seem settled and contented with their farms and herds, they are ready at any hour of any day or night, to seize their swords and battleaxes and soak the soil of England with her native blood. Do I put the matter truly as it stands?'

'As it stands?' said the Queen.

Again a murmur, and this time a nodding of the white heads gave the answer.

The King went on. 'Councillors, there are two strong foreign powers contending with each other for our England. They are already at war with each other. As you know, Alonso landed a large force on the coast beside the mouth of the Nijn intending to attack the Vikings in their thorp, but the Viking army was there before them, awaiting them on the islands of the marshes, and met the Christians with the fury for which they are justly infamous. A third of his Army of the Redeemed was wiped out. Still Alonso will not give up. A detachment of his, an advance guard, had before then taken in a merciless onslaught the Viking Castle of Yggdrasil—where some of his monks had earlier suffered death and humiliation—and there he has established a command centre.'

The arrow tapped the place low on the south-eastern coast where, more or less, the Castle of Yggdrasil stood.

'There his army—newly reinforced with young men from all parts of Europe eager to fight under the banner of the Cross—is now camped. Or the greater part of it. He has stationed a thousand men further north, on the southern and western borders of the Earldom of Felldown.'

The arrow traced the borders.

'The Earl himself has retreated to his cousin of Cornwall, leaving his land open to Alonso. But Alonso does not want to seem hostile to the English lords. He will march through our realm to battle with the Vikings, but declares he will not occupy it if he is not attacked. So long as his soldiers are brought their levied share of provender from the farms, he will leave the farmers unmolested. He wants our good will. And—well, these are the conditions I mentioned to you that we would have to fulfill—if we will agree to build a thousand more churches in Mercia, he will leave us in peace. So, Councillors, the easiest thing for us to do is agree to build the churches and watch Alonso drive the Vikings out of England. Let him unite the islands. And then ...' the King's voice rose for the first time, ringing out the next words, '*then* by cunning and strength, wrest power from him. That is a plan we could decide on without dread. As I say, it would be easy at first. The struggle would come later. But ...' He held a moment of silence, then said very quietly, 'It assumes that Alonso will win the war against the Vikings.'

'Against the Vikings,' the Queen repeated.

The King turned to face the Duke.

'Tell us, Bassington, how likely is it that the Army of the Redeemed will win the war against the Vikings?'

'Majesty,' said the Duke of Bassington, resting the golden arrow on his shoulder, 'I would wager five to two that the Vikings will win the war.'

'And I will not take the wager,' the King said, 'because I would wager the same.'

The Councillors shifted uneasily in their polished oak chairs.

'What then, you're wondering?' said the King. 'Indeed. What then?'

There was silence in the room. The Councillors looked at the King, expecting him to answer his question. The King looked from face to face of his Councillors, hoping one of them would have the answer he lacked. The Duke of Bassington tapped his arrow on his palm. The two servants holding up the map shifted their positions to ease the strain.

At last Councillor Cuthburd spoke.

'Majesty, Crispin my son has returned from Linkard, bringing news. It may be something we need to take into account. Is it your pleasure that we bring him in?'

'Yes, yes. Let us hear what he has to tell us.'

Councillor Cuthburd fetched in his son, who had been waiting impatiently in the next room, trying to think of a rhyme for 'goddess'. He made his personally designed bow first to his sovereign and then, with even more elaborate gestures, to his sovereign's lady, who smiled indulgently.

'Begin!' the King commanded.

'Majesties! I hear from the Earl of Linkard and the Queens of the Fenreach … wait!'

'Get on with it,' said the King.

'Pardon me, Majesty, but I must start again. I bear a message from just one of the Queens, though the other Queen, and the Earl, and Lady Jessica—she's the Earl's daughter—a very beautiful lady—

'Get on with it,' said the Queen.

'If it please your Majesties, I think my message will make more sense if I can deliver it whole, and in order, if you will be so gwacious as to permit me,'

'Your message? They sent me a message?'

'They did. And it is this. Their strength is even less than they had expected it to be. The Welsh contingent that was due to join them reached England but turned back. Why, no one knows. Now they have learnt that Alonso de Llama intends to march through their lands and fall upon the Vikings in their seasonal settlement, seeking revenge for his defeat at the battle of the Nijn.'

'We know that. That's not new to us. We have received a report of the Abbot's change of plan. Are *we* now being appealed to for reinforcements by *them*?'

'Were you informed, Majesty, that the Viking village has been abandoned except for a few old men, and that all the fighters have gone north to join the main body of the army?'

'No, I did not know that. So what does the Queen want us to do? Get that information to Alonso? So he won't have cause to encroach on their lands?'

'She didn't say so, Majesty.'

'Then what is her message?'

Crispin closed his eyes to concentrate on the words he had been forced by Queen Lily to memorize, and repeated: 'The united English forces will seek an alliance with the Vikings against the invading Army of the Wedeemed.'

There was a long silence.

'That's all?' King Aelfrid said. 'That's the whole message?'

'That's the message, Majesty. I have to tell you it is from Queen Lily. But she wants you to know that the Earl and Queen Bertha agree with it.'

The white heads of the Councillors turned this way and that as they murmured to each other.

They fell silent when the King spoke. 'Well' he said, 'this is a most welcome message. And the wonder of it is, it's the very thing I was about to say myself, that we would be best served by entering into a treaty of alliance with the Vikings.'

The Councillors stared at him, dumbfounded.

The Queen turned towards him slowly with a look of questioning surprise.

'Yes!' said the King. 'I knew it would seem at first a wild idea. But it is the only answer. Because the chances that the Vikings will win the war against the Pope's army stand at five to two. Right, Bassington?'

'Right.'

'And we know,' Councillor Cuthburd said, the first among his peers to grasp the good sense of the proposal, 'that the Vikings can be trusted to abide by a treaty because the Earl of Linkard has had a treaty with the Vikings on his border for years, and they have never broken it. Once it seemed that a Viking had broken it, and he was sentenced to death after trial in the Earl's court, but it turned out he had been the victim of a treacherous plot by another Viking, and no breach of the treaty had been intended, so he was spared.'

'You are very well informed, Councillor,' the King said.

'I pick these stories up from servants' gossip,' the Councillor said.

'So you think my idea is a good one?'

'*Your* idea? Oh yes, Majesty. I think your idea is a very good one'

'Do you all agree with Councillor Cuthburd?'

'It makes perfect sense,' one of the old men said.

'It's the only thing to do,' said another.

And the general murmur was clearly now a noise of assent, as the white heads nodded.

The King turned back to Crispin. 'Did the Queen say anything else at all?' he asked.

'Well,' Crispin's face reddened. 'She did say—she said—I was to tell you not to send me to talk to the Vikings.'

'She said that? And did she say who should be sent?'

'No, only not me.'

'We will send … Bassington,' the King decided.

'Bassington,' the Queen concurred.

'Yes, we will send you, Bassington. You will go and talk directly to—what is the name of the Commander of the Viking forces?'

'Tostig son of Tostig,' Bassington replied promptly.

'To him. Soldier to soldier. You are also well

informed, Bassington. Do you pick up your information from servant's gossip?'

'No, Majesty. I made it my business to find out who was commanding the Viking forces when I heard they were coming to England to fight a war. Now you are sending me to make an alliance with them? I must warn you, Majesty, that an alliance with the Vikings has its dangers.'

'We know we must be cautious. But yes, we are sending you to persuade them that together we will drive Alonso and his invaders out of England, leaving it to us and them, with whom we have no quarrel. Until ...'

His listeners waited.

'Until we are so strong that we will not only recover power over our eastern lands, but can extend our rule over the whole of England, stopping only at the borders of Cornwall, Wales, and Scotland.'

'Cornwall, Wales, and Scotland,' said the Queen.

A Councillor asked, 'Do you mean, Majesty, that we ourselves can become strong enough to drive the Vikings out of England?'

'I do. But not yet. Not next year or the year after that, but yes, in time that is what we must do. Drive them out—or let those who want to stay accept our rule. They are not invincible. But the first step is to rid ourselves of the menace of Alonso de Llama's army of conquest. We will not send our treasure to Rome. We will not bow under the yoke of Rome. It may be that a united England will only be achieved by our sons. Or by their sons. But we are the ones to set the goal. All England under one rule, under English rule, under our rule. But you will say nothing of that to the Vikings, eh, Bassington!'

'Certainly not, Majesty.'

No fault was found with 'the King's plan', or with his great aim of ruling all England. It was agreed that no word of their intentions should be dropped to anyone outside the walls of the throne room. The two holders of the map were made to swear an oath that they would keep what they'd heard secret.

The Duke of Bassington set out at once with a small group of officers for Barleyfield Monastery.

a duel to the death

Gus let Maelstrom make his way sure-footed through the forest towards his home. He was thinking what he would say to Lily, what she would say to him. Would he dare go straight up to her and embrace her?

He would have to judge by how she looked when she saw him—happy, or cross that he had borrowed her horse.

She would have discovered Maelstrom's absence hours ago. And she would have guessed that it was he who had taken her beloved horse. She would think to herself, 'Gus is back! The only person Maelstrom would go with willingly is Gus.' She would be happy—*they* would be happy.

His heart beat faster at the thought of seeing her again. He had planned to go to Goosegarth first, and explain his strange predicament to her: how Mordec had punished him for shutting him up in a burning ship and leaving him to die, by forbidding him to fight with the Viking army. But here he was, ready to fight against the Army of the Redeemed anyway—as a lone fighter, like Sir Baz the lone knight.

He would have asked her then to lend him a horse—Roman Ruin, perhaps, the horse he had ridden when they had raced against each other, she on

Maelstrom winning the race with ease. But when he had come to the stables, which stood at a fair distance from the homestead, he could not resist going inside and looking at the horses—at Maelstrom in particular. And Maelstrom had let him stroke his nose and pat his neck; and had let him put a saddle and reins on him; and mount him; and had responded to the light double-tap of his heels by walking out into the early sunshine, and had quickened his pace into a canter, and was headed to where Gus had left his arms hidden in the clearing where later he had taken Mordec.

Mordec! He had save his life once again. Saving a life makes up for trying to destroy that life, doesn't it?

He would tell Lily the story and she would—

Maelstrom stopped abruptly, and whinnied. Why? Gus's heels tapped, and tapped harder, but the horse would not take another step. Gus looked to see if there was something ahead that the horse did not want to approach.

There was something.

About twenty paces away stood a man in armour and helmet, with his sword in his hand. He was on a slight rise in the ground between the trees, long beams of sunlight slanting down behind him so bright that he was nothing more to Gus's eyes than the black shape of a man. He did not move, but stood, feet planted well apart, sword raised and shin-ing, uttering not a word, not a sound.

'Greetings!' Gus called.

The man did not answer. He stood still, balanced, ready to fight.

Gus sat calmly in the saddle. He would not shirk a fight, but perhaps the man was expecting someone else.

'Should I take off my helmet, let him see my face?' he asked himself. 'He would hear me more clearly too—that I offer greetings, not a challenge.'

But he quickly dismissed the idea. 'No. That would be rash.'

If the man attacked, he would want to waste time replacing his helmet.

He tried calling again, no threat in his tone. 'Will you let me pass?'

Still the warrior neither moved nor spoke. Gus could tell from the outline of the helmet that this was not a Viking. And he surely was not one of Alonso's army come before the rest. Alonso's army carried round shields. This warrior carried none.

'Who are you?' he asked more loudly. 'What is it you want of me?'

The man took a step forward, began to descend the low rise, and held his sword out towards the horse. Gus could not, would not, let Maelstrom be hurt. He would turn off to the side, away from this sinister aggressor. He pulled on the reins to turn the horse, but Maelstrom whinnied again, shook his head, pulled back against Gus's strength, and would not move.

Hastily Gus dropped to the ground. He must go and meet the attacker. His sword was out in a moment, and holding it ready to strike, he stepped forward cautiously but threateningly, watching for the next move his opponent would make, ready to respond as his fighter's instinct and his long training would direct him.

But with sudden speed the man came running, bringing his sword from far back, over and down on to Gus's leather-armoured shoulder, splitting it open.

'So that is how it is to be!' Gus yelled. 'Right, then. We fight to the death!'

He was soon all too sure that his opponent was as good a swordsman as he was himself. Gus grunted, and, as Vikings did, he shrieked. They sidestepped in a circle, their hidden eyes fixed on each other; neither pausing for a moment; attacking, defending, attacking again.

Gus's lunges became swifter, his cuts harder. His mysterious enemy in black metal armour and helmet did the same, his sword flashing like Thor's lightning, its clash on Gus's sword the only sound that came from him. All he expressed was fury, and Gus understood with cold certainty—here was a man intent on killing.

Right! So be it! Gus was as intent on killing him, just as ruthlessly, just as certainly—stranger though he was, attacking for no reason Gus could imagine. One or the other of them would die today, any moment now, here in the forest.

Unable to drive the silent warrior back, Gus thought he would use a tactic which had often succeeded for him in his duels. He began to retreat, drawing the man towards him, and leaning down a little so as to seize a favourable moment for an upward thrust under the man's chain mail and into his belly or his heart.

But at that moment luck worked against him and for his opponent.

As he brought his back foot forward to make the plunge, it caught on a tree root humping up out of the leafy ground, and he fell, face down, an intense pain shooting through his ankle. In a moment he had rolled over onto his back, his sword pointing at the man's heart—but it was stopped by the metal, and the point of the other's sword was pricking his own bare throat. He felt the sticky heat of blood beginning to ooze round the side of his neck, and his right arm weaken as if it too was bleeding. One more thrust by that ruthless hand and he would die!

The man put a foot on his chest and straitened into a position from which he could put his utmost power into a killing thrust. Now!

Now it would happen!

Surely he was not hesitating? This was not a moment for weighing life against death.

Gus's thoughts raced: 'I am dying in combat. I will go to Valhalla. It is good. It is the death I always wanted. Though it has come too soon. What is he waiting for? Does he want to make it slow? Does he want to torture me? Why? What has he got against me? Who is he? Who in my short life have I so offended? Only Mordec, and this is not Mordec. I will ask him.'

'Mordec?' he mumbled, thick-tongued, and could say no more as only a gurgling sound came out of his throat.

But as if he had said a magic word, the sword was taken away from the wound. It fell to the ground and a pair of gauntlets dropped one on the other beside it.

Hands were lifting off his helmet. They had to raise his head to do it, and with the bending forward his throat felt the pain of the cut so acutely, he squeezed his eyes shut to help him bear it.

Someone was speaking his name. 'Gus,' the voice said. 'Gus.'

He could not think who it might be. Gently his head was laid down again, on a heap of leaves piled up to form a pillow. He heard the sound of fabric tearing, and then the hands were binding his wound, carefully lifting his head again, carefully laying it down on the soft damp pillow.

He opened his eyes and thought he saw Lily looking down at him. Was she dead too? How had she come here? Had the silent warrior killed her too? Then they would be together with the gods.

His strong arm reached for her and drew her down upon him. Her face pressed to his chest, her hair spread over his mouth, her bloodstained hands held his head—holding him to this world. Slowly she raised herself and put her lips very softly on his.

saved by the bell

It was Mel de Gustybuss himself, to whom the bad news came on wings, who took it to Captain Anwid at Goosegarth.

The Queens welcomed him.

'You bring us news?' Queen Bertha asked.

'Bad news, I'm very sorry to have to say,' Mel replied, and as Captain Anwid, the person he had brought it to, was standing beside them, he sensibly waited not a moment longer to deliver it. 'The King of Cornwall will not be marching to the aid of Mercia. Sadly, Captain, King Mark was captured, and hope that he is still alive has now been abandoned. He was sailing from his island to where his troops were assembled on the border with England to start them on their march to Mercia, when the dreaded pirate Bjarwulf seized his ship. All on board the royal ship were taken captive, and all but the King and one of his servants were bound and thrown overboard. At first it was believed that the King was being held for ransom, but then came the news that he had fought Bjarwulf to the death—and lost the fight.'

'And my father?' Anwid gasped, clutching Mel's arm. 'Was he …?'

'Ah no, no, Captain, he is alive, he is well. He was not on board the King's ship. Only … no one is quite sure where he is. He set off with a small retinue to return to his earldom, believing it was a mistake ever to have left it, and that as long as he was there neither the Christians nor the Vikings would take it.'

Captain Anwid wasted not a moment. Before Mel had finished speaking she was on a run to the stables, calling to her girls to saddle their horses or put them between the shafts of their carts. Within the hour they were on their way to Felldown.

They rode hard, having no mercy on the horses. Their way was south over grassland, down the margin of the forests of Mercia.

They stopped neither to eat nor drink, until the dark fell and made them pause.

They entered the forest, where wolves and thieves were known to prowl—so many thieves of so terrible a reputation that the law of Mercia had long since given up trying to extend its arm into these bosky haunts—and laid themselves down on the rough ground under the oaks.

They drank sparely from their flagons; cracked open raw eggs snatched in handfuls of straw from under the hens at Goosegarth and poured the slithery contents down their parched throats. And while some kept watch, turn and turn about, they let themselves sleep for a few hours.

At the crack of dawn on they rode, furiously, relent-lessly, though the sun rose high and the sweat broke out on the horses, and their own sweat dimmed their eyes.

When they reached the north bank of the River Tamesis, rain began to fall though the sun still shone.

They threw back their heads and opened their mouths for the water to strike their tongues as they rode on, and they shivered with joy for the coolness as their soaked tunics clung to their skins.

The rain stopped before they reached the first bridge on the edge of London. Once over the river, they had to slow their pace, for the road was busy with other riders, other carts, and labourers walking with tools over their shoulders, and women with burdens, and raggedly clothed barefooted children with hunger and mischief in their eyes.

When they had but a short way more to go until they could turn into the meadows of Felldown, they looked for the towers of Cogg Hall and soon they saw them looming through the haze of the afternoon.

They advanced cautiously, but there was no sign of occupation of the land by the Christian army; no tents, no noise.

Earl Botham was not to be found in his castle.

Anwid's voice calling 'Father! Father!' echoed through the halls and no answer came. She could feel her heart beating hard with trepidation as she hurried towards the tenants' cottages to ask if anyone had seen him.

Her girls went off in all directions seeking news of him.

She found him herself seated on a barrel in a barn with a crowd of his tenants. She observed with approval that he had thought to clothe himself and his attendants like labourers. It meant he wasn't being too foolhardy, too careless.

When he saw Anwid bearing down on him, shaking her head, and half smiling—a look of exasperation mixed with relief, he rose happily to his feet and spread wide his arms.

'M'dear!' he called. 'This is a nice surprise! What brings you here?'

'You,' said Anwid.

They embraced warmly. It was not their custom to show so much affection for each other—although both of them always felt it. The times were changing them.

'You are not supposed to be here, Father. The Christian army is still camped somewhere near by. If they know you have returned …'

'They don't know, and these good fellows won't tell them. I came actually to see what they had to say about coming under new management, so to speak. It troubled me rather that I had left without informing them about it, and hearing their point of view.'

'And now you have?'

'They were just telling me.'

'And what is it?'

They say they're happy to stay. They say they're all Christians, and if the Abbot allows them to stay in their cottages and carry on as always, that's what they'll do. Right, my good men?'

'Yes. Right' the voices murmured or called out.

'And you, Father? What will you do?'

'I'll take Mark's place. I'll lead his soldiers against the Christians, along with Aelfrid's army. I have my armour and our pennants hidden not far away. The men I brought with me are all fine fellows, keen to fight.'

Then the Earl walked out of the barn and quietly wept.

He had been very fond of his cousin Mark. He had even hoped that the King might become his son-in-law. He had let himself envision a grandson of his becoming the King of both Cornwall and a united England and joining the two realms into one kingdom.

But it was not for the disappointment of his dream that he wept. It was for Mark himself.

He hung his head to hide his tears from his daughter. She saw them anyway, and proffered him the pocket handkerchief she had used to mop her brow on the furious ride to save her father from death at the hands of Abbot Alonso. He gently pushed away the hand that held it and wiped his cheeks with the back of his own hand.

'We two will lead his men into battle,' he said. 'You and I.'

'And my gels will fight with the men,' she said.

'Let's go,' he said.

Neither of them noticed that one of the monks Abbot Alonso had posted to keep watch for 'intruders' had seen them, and was hurrying towards the church, to ring its bell and summon soldiers, who would put an end forever to the Earldom of Felldown.

The monk arrived panting on the grassy knoll. He hurried to the base of the bell-tower, he seized the rope, he pulled on it, the great bell moved, to and fro, heavy and slow—but not a sound came out of it. He pulled harder. He brought the rope lower, his arms strained—why was the tongue not touching the metal sides and sending out a great toll that would be heard for miles over the countryside?

'Look, Father, look!' said Anwid, pointing to the bell tower as they approached it.

'What is it? What's happening?'

'The bell is swinging far out, far out, but it isn't ringing … because … come, let's run and see … I can see now, it is because the tongue has been wrapped up to silence it. One of Alonso's monks must be trying to summon the soldiers, but we are saved, Father … the bell won't ring.'

They found the monk still striving, reaching high up with both hands on the rope, and bending far down in useless effort to sound the alarm. Anwid leapt upon him, her dagger aimed at his throat. He let go the rope. The bell went on swinging as he fell, his eyes opening wide in astonishment at the inexplicable and the unexpected befalling him in the last moment of his life.

'Well done, Captain!' the Earl said.

But Anwid did not hear him. Her attention was wholly absorbed in watching a strange thing happening in the top of the bell tower. The thick bundle of cloth that had kept the tongue from sounding against the metal of the bell was slowly unwinding itself. A pair of legs appeared under it. They gripped the rope and slid down it, the bundle with them, and last

came a head—the pretty head of girl, who laughed
as she jumped the last few feet to the ground, shook
out the wrappings to fall to her ankles—layers of
woollen skirts of many colours—and bowed like the
entertainer she was at the end of the performance.

'Charlotte!'

It was the dancer herself.

Anwid burst into laughter, partly with relief, and
partly at the sight of Charlotte. 'You look like a dome
with half a doll on top,' she said, as she embraced
her friend.

Charlotte had not left Cogg Hall. She told them
how she'd entertained the tenants for her dinners; had
slept in Anwid's bed—and had watched the watching monks.

She noticed they took it in turns to patrol the hall
and grounds, so she had only one at a time to keep
a watch on.

She knew that the ringing of the bell would bring
Abbot Alonso's soldiers to occupy the hall and steal
the lands, until Alonso himself came to take the Earl's
place and rob him of all he owned.

She had made a plan and tested it: How many
woollen layers would muffle the tongue of the bell?
How best could she cling firmly and long enough
to its rod as it swung? How would she hide her legs
under the skirts? She tried until she succeeded.

She would not let the warning bell ring.

When she had finished her tale—murmuring it as
they huddled under the eaves of the church—Anwid
hurried to summon the platoon of girls and the Earls'

attendants, and get the horses saddled and the carts loaded with supplies. The tenants—still loyal to the Earl though willing to accept a new master—brought bread and wine, wheat and oil, from their larders and barns.

Weapons were taken down from the walls of Cogg Hall.

Before dark they were on their way—without Charlotte.

Anwid wanted her to come with them. 'Or what will become of you?' she said.

'I'll always be safe,' Charlotte replied brightly.

'Yes, I think you will,' Anwid agreed. Someone as resourceful as the dancer would not easily be caught.

The Earl and his men, Anwid and her girls, travelled first along the shore to avoid being seen by the Christian soldiers camped on the southern border of Felldown.

They turned inland to give a wide berth to the lands of Yggdrasil, where the bulk of the Christian army was camped and preparing to invade Mercia, but kept moving south-west toward the border of England and Cornwall, where the Cornish army waited to be led into battle.

the great battle

More is known about the Mercian War than any other of the many wars fought in England before the reign of King Arthur. This is because it was chronicled at length by Father Denis Donlock of Linkard, and in part by Dellibeth, Countess of Felldown. Further information is to be found in the archives of Harald Goldmountain at the Gaudin School of Science, War and Engineering; in the letters of Queen Aethylwynne to her nephew Crispin Cuthburd preserved in the library of Tamworth Palace; and in the useful if not entirely trustworthy Saga of Tostig, still sung by the skalds in the mead halls of the Northlands. Finally, and arguably most valuably, there are the many tales told of Mordec, including those reputed to have been told by himself and handed down by word of mouth 'in his own words'.

* * *

It really did seem that Alonso de Llama, Commander-in-the-field of the Army of the Redeemed, had never for a moment anticipated, or entertained the possibility, that the English would mount an offensive against his troops.

He had fully expected the Mercians to make a show of defending their territory at the approach of Alonso's hordes marching north through the centre of their country; but he expected that when he had parleyed with the King, and with the various kings and queens and earls of smaller states—many of them little more than big farms—they would, every one of them, agree to his perfectly reasonable terms: merely that they build churches and pay taxes to Rome. So obviously were those modest requirements better than being killed and having their lands seized, no sane ruler would refuse them.

What he was unsure about, as he rode at the head of his marching men, was at what point the Vikings would appear before his troops and the great battle begin.

He had learnt that there were no Vikings in their seasonal settlement on the Linkard border, and that the entire Viking army was now camped north of Mercia; that the Vikings intended to engage his forces, stop his campaign, and send the Army of the Redeemed back to France.

So he had developed a third plan—march to do battle with the Vikings again, but this time with overwhelming numbers of men.

Reports of the Viking numbers had varied so much he could not rely on any of them. But the highest count had come to fewer than his hundred thousand men.

The Army of the Redeemed camped for the last night of their march some miles east of Tamworth, and though Alonso set heavy guard in four-hour watches on all sides, even on the east along the edge of the forest where the danger came more from beasts then men, it was only from the north that he expected the enemy's approach, and there he stationed twenty rows of swordsmen backed by a wide curve of archers.

Throughout a moonless the night the camp fires burned, throwing flickering shadows on the wall of trees. 'Such great warriors they are supposed to be, the Vikings, and we felt their ruthless fury at the Nijn, but clever enough to attack us at our most vulnerable in the night—that they are not,' Alonso thought. He wanted to find reason to despise them since they had defeated his first battalions so completely, so horribly. They had humiliated the army of the Pope.

He could think of no reason for their absence on this night. He sent no scouts to search in any direction. He guessed that Viking eyes were watching his fires and counting the dark forms of soldiers round them from the higher branches of the forest oaks. But it did not cross his mind to fear that over the low hills and along the small river beds and across the meadows fanning out from Tamworth—where in the ivy-covered palace King Aelfrid and Queen Aethelwynne sat in state on their thrones all through the night receiving reports from spies shod in woolly sheepskin—tens of Mercians, men and boys (and seven girls dressed like boys) were keeping watch. They lay low in the thick grass, lurked in the orchards, hunched in the ditches and the hedges, keeping their eyes on his resting army, and on the black silk tent in which he sat and brooded, and fitfully lay down now and then to sleep uneasily. He would wake as if startled by a sudden loud noise. But there was no sudden loud noise. The soldiers obeyed his orders to be quiet as best they could unless to raise the alarm for an attack. No owls hooted in the forest on that unusual night. They too were keeping watch with their big round eyes.

Alonso would not admit to himself that he was afraid. He *knew* that the sheer numbers of his army would be enough to overwhelm the Vikings and keep the English submissive.

Why then, he demanded silently of the black sky, cannot I get the rest I need to strengthen me for the coming battle? And from time to time he prayed for victory, and ended his prayer by kissing a wooden crucifix on which the figure of his god was carved and gilded and which he wore under his garments near to his heart, hung on a gold chain.

* * *

Mordec slept well in the soft bed of the abbot of Barleyfield Monastery; better than he had slept on Harald Goldmountain's ship, when the nights were aloud with the snores of the great man. As Harald had chosen to continue living on his ship in the harbour, and Commander Tostig chose to sleep as always on his campaign stretcher in the monks' dormitory along with his officers, the wide and airy chamber of the abbot, with its oak furniture, rich cloths, and downy bed was left to Mordec. He had offered it to his father, but Hauk preferred to stay in a tent with old comrades-in arms who recalled with him the good old days of past campaigns, in particular Olaf the Shipbuilder and Harvald the Armourer, father of Horsa the lost.

Mordec had parted that night, quite early, from Harald and the Commander and Daedalus, after a final and careful look over their plans—as co-ordinated earlier with the Duke of Bassington's. The Commander had asked Mordec, casually, why he thought the fertile grass fields of northern Mercia were as empty of farms as he had reported they were. And Mordec had suddenly known the answer.

'They are too often crossed by our raids to the west and north for farmers to risk their herds on them,' he had replied. The Commander had smiled, and Harald Goldmountain had laughed his great laugh, which woke a good many of the men already in their beds.

No new information had come in that required them to change anything. There was no reason why they should not sleep soundly. And the Commander reminded Mordec that he liked his soldiers to have a good night's sleep before a battle.

Leif slept deeply on a smaller bed under the triple-arched window. He had demanded that Mordec ask him formally for permission to go into the danger of battle.

'Ah, yes, of course, please permit me, my owner,' Mordec had said as he laid his weapons in a row on the floor under the portraits of former abbots hung on the paneled wall.

Sword, battleaxe, dagger. Next came the chainmail, and finally the helmet that Daedalus had designed for him. The metal arched forward over his face, allowing space for his eyeglasses. It resembled the face of the legendary and fearsome beaked bear (*ramphiarctos*) that travellers told of and which was sometimes used as a figurehead on pirate ships—a resemblance that its maker had increased by painting flaring red nostrils on the black metal and a row of sharp white teeth.

Leif's leather armour and short sword came next in the row. His assignment during the battle was to guard Harald Goldmountain's ship, along with six of the crew.

Neither of them woke until the church bell tolled an hour before dawn, as Commander Tostig had ordered.

* * *

Miles away, Captain Anwid and her girls slept well too, rolled in blankets on the ground, in the manner they had slept in happier times on the deck of The Good Ship Good.

Earl Botham lay on a bundle of hay, of which his horse took a mouthful now and then.

His solemn last words of the evening to his companions had been: 'Tomorrow we reach the southern shore and start eastward to the Cornish border. After only one night's rest we will lead the Cornishmen northward and fall upon Alonso's men wherever we find them. We will be merciless. This is no time for restraint, my good friends, no time for restraint. And when Alonso has been defeated we will join with our fellow Englishmen to drive the Vikings from these islands. A Viking killed my cousin Mark, King of Cornwall. I will have my revenge. Ten thousand men will follow us. With such an army we will not fail.'

A quiet cheer, uttered more in sympathy than confidence, went up from Anwid and her girls.

But Anwid said softly to Dellibeth as they wrapped themselves in their blankets and chose grassy spots to lie upon, 'To Father the future always looks bright. I wish I could be as sure as he is that we will not fail.'

* * *

Earl Reginald of Linkard dozed upright in his chair behind the table of the counting-house.

The small pillow under his head and the woollen rug over his knees had been put in place gently by Mel de Gustybuss, who was staying awake to keep an eye on his master.

The Earl had not meant to fall asleep at all. Though he felt less helpless now that he was part of the strong military alliance King Aelfrid had formed with the Vikings, he did not feel it was safe to fall asleep. He did not trust Alonso to wait until morning to advance, and the defence of his earldom and the Fenreach was still largely in his own hands. But weariness had crept over him and he dreamt unhappily of reports that he could not comprehend.

Now as real reports came in from their spies, Father Donlock received them on the drawbridge of the palace.

They were brought to him by elderly Vikings, the men who had stayed behind when the rest had gone north to join the army camped round Barleyfield Monastery.

The old men moved through the familiar forest without attracting attention, and some rode quite far to the south and relayed news of the invaders' movements.

Father Donlock would give the reports to the Earl as soon as he waked. Father Donlock had long since chosen where to bestow his loyalty; not to the distant Pope in Rome despite his priestly vows, but to the man in the counting-house, his daughter in her bower, and the people round him in this green and pleasant land where he'd been born.

* * *

The bell of Barleyfield tolled. The Viking high command awoke.

Leif woke, and seeing that Mordec's eyes were still closed, he knelt on the bed beside him and tried to roll up one of the closed eyelids with a careful forefinger. It opened, and so did the other, and there lay a wakened Mordec smiling at Leif, then jerking up with a roar, sending Leif off the bed and on to the floor.

'A Viking will never be taken in his sleep,' he said, laughing. 'We have an inner watchman and one touch will release the berserker in us. That's what I am now. That's what I will be in battle. You have pulled the string and bent me like a bow, Leif son of Nameless. I thank you for it.'

When Mordec stood before him in full armour with the weird and terrifying helmet on—which Leif had not seen before—he paid Mordec the compliment of a long low whistle.

* * *

The King of Mercia rose from his throne and solemnly gave orders to his commander, the Duke of Bassington, who received them without argument since he had taught them to his sovereign the night before.

* * *

Dawn broke.

Captain Anwid shed her blanket, shook her girls awake. Earl Botham's guards saddled his horse.

* * *

The Army of the Redeemed rose in their thousands and tens of thousands and stood waiting, rank on rank, for the command to advance.

To show their readiness and eagerness, every man had a hand on his sword.

Alonso was glad of the strong arm that helped him up into his saddle.

He was the only man mounted. In front of them all Alonso faced his troops, then turned his horse so he sat with his back to them and raised his right arm—they saw the metal on his forearm glint in the early sunshine—and slowly lowered it to point northward.

173

That was the command.

He started forward, and the thousands upon thousands of men in red tunics with white crosses over chainmail, followed him towards the field of their coming glorious victory or their deaths.

They did not march to the beat of drums.

Some but not all of them chanted in unison, dirge-like chants with Latin words.

They bore no flags. But at both ends of every fiftieth row a cross was held high. The bearers of the crosses handed their burdens over to fresh bearers after every pause for rest.

Alonso began to feel a hot eagerness, which made him also feel strong. It was, he chose to believe, a passion for spreading the Christian message of peace and hope, or at least the saving power of the blessed Church of Christ, that drove him forward with almost rapturous zeal.

But he was an introspective man, a man who debated much with himself, and he knew, without liking it, that what made his heart beat faster as he approached the hour of battle was … hatred; hatred of the Vikings, who flourished so proudly and carelessly in this world, who did not feel that they were a moral offence in the eyes of God, and who never seemed to suffer for their pride and sinfulness. He could not leave them to their ultimate just punishment in Hell. He wanted them to understand now, in this life, that they were doomed to eternal pain. He wanted to see the dread and horror in the eyes—the eyes behind the glasses of that Mordec, that murderer who had got away with his foul deed committed in the very church of Alonso's own abbey.

Where were they?

How long would they hold back, the Vikings with blood lust in their eyes and battleaxes raised above their heads? How long before he'd hear their shrieking and gargling battle cries?

'Come, come on,' Alonso called silently to them as he pressed ahead, with his thousands of warriors behind him as though he pulled them after him as lightly and inevitably as the Mother of God drew her train of heavenly blue after her when she walked at evening across the glittering floors of Heaven.

The forest on his right came to an abrupt end. There was open grassland stretching away to the horizon on his left, and ahead of him there was a rise in the ground, a grassy ridge—and there, yes at last, there *they* were, Vikings on their horses, men in metal on strong steeds watching him advance. He raised his arm straight up. His army halted. There was a moment of pause that seemed much longer. Time was suspended, all held still, except that Alonso's heart beat hard, hard, under the metal of his breast.

No heralds were sent from either side with white banners aflutter to parley. What was there to say? Each side knew all that this was about. It was about killing. It was about death. It was about soaking this field with blood. It was about the saving of England, whether it would be from sin or from tocsins and taxes.

Alonso brought his arm down to point forward. He thrilled to hear the great shout that arose from the thousands of throats behind him. His soldiers ran as best they could in their armour, a tide of red and white bobbing and surging forward behind, beside, beyond their leader—who was swinging his arm now in a circle to hurry them on, forward. Their swords were out, their ranks broke up, their boots stomped down, mashing the grass into the ground. Alonso reined in his horse and waited for the Vikings to descend.

'Now,' he screamed, 'now!' Though whether it was a command to his own soldiers or to the Vikings ranged along the ridge, he hardly knew himself, only that now, now, the moment was busting burst upon them.

But the Vikings were not descending upon them, thundering down on galloping hooves, their battle-axes raised above their heads. Why?

Alonso's horse stood still as the tide of men swept past it and on to the rise, those in front compelled to advance faster and faster by the multitude coming on behind them, though the ground became steep, and they strained to look up as they climbed, panting, and saw—no horseman now standing above them. Instead there was a row of giant wooden structures, and one after another, and some together, with a grating noise, were flinging rocks at the body of men behind the climbers, and something scalding hot and thick and black was pouring down upon the climbers themselves.

They dropped their faces to let the hot liquid flow over their metal helmets, but it found their necks and flowed under their collars down their backs under their useless armour, blistering their skin. They shrieked as they fell, by the dozen, by the hundred. And behind them the soldiers were turning in all directions, pushing each other as they dodged the avalanche of rocks, stepping over the bodies of those knocked to the green-brown earth, the blood-red earth. They knocked Alonso's horse to the ground. The Abbot struggled to rise to his feet, both arms above his head holding off, pushing away panicked men who knew not which way to flee.

When the ranks still far from the rise saw and understood that their front ranks were moving chaotically, that their leader had disappeared in the melee, that danger was falling from above, they slowed and stopped, so a wide space was opened between the front and the bulk of the army.

It was then, on Bassington's command, that the troops of Mercia fell upon the Christians' left flank, taking them so much by surprise that it was almost an hour before the Mercians were set upon by any considerable number of the Redeemed.

The fighting became fierce, and the footsoldiers of Mercia would have been quite overwhelmed, had not Bassington's horsemen plunged at a fierce gallop into the tail of the Christian horde, and trampled down, and decapitated many—though some of the invaders struck a Mercian from his mount here and there, and of those some were run through by a Christian sword.

Then the Christians began to aim their swords at the legs and breasts of the horses, and brought many a Mercian rider down to his death. Some of the steeds reared and whinnied, tossing their riders on to the swords of the foe. But as the Christians tried to defend themselves from the greater danger of the horsemen, the Mercian footsoldiers rallied and attacked again.

The sheer numbers of the Army of the Redeemed would have made certain of victory for the Church of Christ, as Alonso had anticipated, if the battle had continued as it was between them and the Mercians. But now on the right flank of the Christian army lines of men with feathers in their helmets, blue, red and some of them yellow, emerged from the forest and hurled themselves into the fray.

They were followed by a small but determined force, on foot and armed with short bows, a small, lethal battalion from Linkard and the Fenreach. On the barked orders of a white knight on a white steed, they shot a hail of arrows into the midst of the Christians, and another, and another, until it seemed that the air was thick with the zinging shafts.

Twenty of the Linkardians were from the Bond House, most of them mere boys, only too happy to have been let out for training with sword and bow, and keen to go to war. They knew no fear. But most of their arrows bounced off the Christians' helmets, and almost all the rest fell to the ground. Still, a few found flesh, delivering a slow death, for the arrows were poisoned.

The main effect of the new attack from the east was to confuse the Christian commanders. They did not know which way to send their strength, from which side their enemy would strike next.

Meanwhile, the great force of the mounted Vikings began their attack over the edge of the Barleyfield height down upon the scattered remnant of Alonso's front ranks. The wooden contraptions that had flung rocks and boiling tar upon them were removed, while a terrible noise arose, of whistling and bird cries, drum-beating growing louder and louder, blood-curdling yodels, screams, screeches, howls, yelps, squeals, dis-cordant notes on trumpets and horns, as wave after wave of mounted Vikings came heaving up over the ridge and bearing down on the scorched and battered Christians, their frightful weapons raised high aloft.

They reaped a harvest of Christian lives as it were in passing, for they swept on into the mass of battling men, their prey easily marked out, every one a target in red and white for blows of the Vikings' battleaxes and their swinging balls of iron with poisoned spikes.

Mordec, peering through glasses and the bars of his bulging helmet, was riding in the midst of the Viking throng full-tilt into the battle. With one strong thrust of his lance, he pushed down a whole row of Christian. The the fine blade of his lance had gone clean through the chest of one and into the chest of another behind him; but as they fell they knocked down three more, and one remained pinned under the corpse of the second man.

Mordec tried to turn his horse, but the beast fell sideways to the ground, its neck pierced by a Christian sword. Mordec leapt from it before he could be pinned to the ground with one leg under it. And at that moment he felt a great fury rise in him, and a far greater strength.

'I am truly a Viking,' his mind shouted, 'born to battle.'

Mordec the reader, Mordec the map-maker, Mordec the dancing prince who had bathed in jasmine, were gone. Mordec half-of-Lombard-blood vanished. He was all Viking, and, sure of his power, he raised his battleaxe and hurled himself into the thick of the fighting. He pounded the earth, his arms wielded his weapon with speed and sureness, and to his own surprise he heard himself bellowing a wordless battle-cry.

Behind the fearsome face-guard of his helmet, behind his glasses, a new Mordec glared out at the world as though he had only to glance at an enemy to kill him.

He knew he could destroy anyone and anything that stood in his way.

He could run faster than a bird could fly.

He was ten feet tall and could put is mighty arms round boulders and lift them out of the grip of the earth, raise them high and fling them at the legions of weak small men coming against him, an indomitable giant standing on the earth, riding it as if he was a god.

If he wasn't a god, he was something almost as terrifying. What he had called himself in a joke for Leif he now became: *a berserker*. The rush of fury and power flushed through him again and again, the moving force of his arms as he laid about him, knocking down enemies as if they could no more stand under his blows than frail saplings rooted in shallow soil.

He was himself a weapon, an instrument of death, striking left and right, unaware that the shrieks of triumph alternating with a gargling sound that he could hear above all the other noises of the battle were issuing from his own throat.

The gargling sound formed a name: 'Alonso!' he roared, 'Alonso you demon, come here!'

He saw things—his father on foot striking low at the legs of a Christian with his battleaxe, Olaf and Gunnar still mounted and bringing their spears straight down behind the shields of the Christians, huge Hakon swinging a spiked ball, felling Christians as fast as a scythe cut barley, Rorick parrying a Christian sword and driving his dagger into the enemy soldier's thigh—that he was to remember later as if recalling a dream, for he was not aware in the moment of seeing anything but enemy targets, head, bodies and limbs, as he slashed his way through clusters of the invaders, until those that still stood upright turned and fled from him, none dared come near him, he stood alone, swinging his battle-axe in a wide arc.

He was about to charge on again, but something he saw stopped him abruptly. His arms dropped to his side and he stood still. The blood did not cease to rush through his veins, his eyes to glare, his heart to pump wildly. His fury did not abate. Rather it intensified, coiled itself up ready to spring, because before him he saw a man marked with the white cross on red, but not a Christian, rather a fellow Viking who had lost his helmet so his face was plain to see. And Mordec knew who he was: Kol son of Knefrod, a man without honour; the man who had played a foul trick on him and brought him close to a horrible and humiliating death.

Though he stood still for a moment looking at Kol, the berserker in his limbs was still there. His fast-coursing blood seemed to be singing within him, his eyes behind metal and glass widened and grew brilliant and fierce, and he laughed as he shouted, 'Thor has delivered you into my hands!'

Kol stood transfixed. He did not want to see the face of the Viking before him. He heard the blood-curdling laughter, he guessed that this man had gone berserk, and he was more afraid than he had ever been in his life.

'Who are you?' he called, putting on a show of bravado that he did not feel, for he was at heart a coward.

'I am your worst nightmare. My name is Mordec son of Hauk. Remember me? I remember you. You are Kol son of Knefrod. You are a traitor not just to me but to all Vikings. You will die now and be the dinner of vultures and wolves and maggots.'

'Mordec? Is it you? Ha! You! You wouldn't dare … you know you cannot beat me …'

The voice trailed off into uncertainty as Mordec, took a step towards him, shifting his battleaxe into his left hand. With his right he drew his sword and took another step, and another, and another—an unstoppable force advancing on its prey.

Kol raised his own sword only to have it struck instantly out of his hand with one swift stroke of Mordec's blade. He began to back away.

'Mordec, don't … don't …' But Mordec was not to be stopped. He flung his sword aside and raised his battleaxe high with both hands, rushed upon Kol and brought the weapon down with twice the normal strength of a man, deep into Kol's skull, cleaving it in two. He chopped off the broken head, and all four of the dead man's limbs. He could not stop. He did not want to stop until there was no more to be done with an axe to the corpse of his enemy. Then he fetched his sword and pierced the limbless trunk, driving the blade deep into it, all the way through to the ground. When he pulled it out again, he had such an intense feeling of having put something right that he laughed aloud with joy.

While Mordec was venting his fury on his personal enemy, the main body of the Vikings—now fronted by footsoldiers—were encountering a reassembled force of Christians.

The invaders were advancing with their swords held out before them, crosses held aloft. The chanting started again. There were very many of them, thousands upon thousands marching and chanting in unison. They broke into a run, and parted, some forward, some eastward, some westward. Their captains shouted the orders, for Alonso de Llama was nowhere to be seen.

The Vikings surged to meet them, spaced apart, which allowed the berserkers among them to break away and fight freely where and how they chose. A moment more and the clash of arms began again.

The battle raged all day. The close fighting had men dancing on the corpses of their comrades and their enemies, and stumbling over the dead or suffering bodies of the horses.

The Viking horsemen who were still mounted looked often towards their Commander for the signal to pause the battle, to retreat, to allow the enemy to follow them up the rise.

In the late afternoon the signal came and the retreat began.

The captains of the Redeemed felt a rise of hope when they saw it and thought their victory was near. They advanced as many men as they could reach with their commands to follow the Vikings, who, they shouted, were fleeing.

'Follow! The field is almost won!' they cried. 'We'll finish them off! Attack them from behind!'

The Vikings urged their bleeding horses up over the rise, and their foot soldiers swarmed after them. The shouting Christians, already drunk with triumph, followed, cutting down some, but also losing some of their own as Vikings turned and fought as if they could never be exhausted.

When the Viking riders, and then the men on foot, had topped the rise, they parted left and right, leaving the way ahead clear. The Christians gathered there, thick on the field, and more and more of them came up. The ground was flat. The sun was sinking and a greyness fell over the land. Still they could see the Vikings huddled together—in fear, the captains thought—some over here and some over there. The Christians were re-formed into long tight battle lines, back to back.

But when they were ready and awaiting the signal to advance on the clusters of Vikings, two great lights burst upon them; one on those facing left and one on those facing right. From both directions a wall of fire advanced smoothly upon them.

'Hold your ground!' the captains cried, for the lines began to break up and many would have rushed back over the ridge. What gave them pause was a line of flame creeping along that edge of the field, all the way along; a line of low flame, and when it had travelled all the way across, it grew upward into another wall of flire. And the two big walls were advancing still, frames covered with torches, moving on a hundred wheels, each wheel turning on a well-greased axle, pushed forward by hundreds of strong men behind each frame.

When the Christians realized what was about to be done to them, many screamed, and many dropped their swords and fell upon their knees and prayed. After some hesitation, the captains did too. Soon all of them were on their knees, and a lamentation rose in the air as the two walls of fire came steadily upon them. And above the screams a tremendous laugh rang out; Harald Goldmountain was exulting in a certainty of victory.

A few hundred Christians chose to escape the closing walls of fire by running through the fire on the edge of the field and rolling down the slope beyond to put the flames out that scorched their legs and arms and burst upon their red chests, consuming the white crosses. Those who survived the burning were finished off with spears and swords by the Mercians waiting for them at the foot of the slope.

Laughing Harald Goldmountain, in gilded armour, seated on a white horse, its purple cloth stained on one side by blood from a wound of its own and not of its master, was in charge of the frame-pushers on the east, while Commander Tostig was behind those on the west. Harald looked about him for Mordec, his favourite, and seeing he was not near, sent men to find him.

They did not find him. They did not even look for him where he was walking, steadily and soberly with a flaming torch in his hand, along the edge of the forest, away from the battle—but not away from the war.

The demon that had possessed his body and mind had departed as soon as he had finished cutting Kol son of Knefred into pieces, had slit open the wretch's trunk from throat to groin, spread his ribcages open wide, like a pair of Christian angels' wings in the pictures on church walls, and mounted the thing on an abandoned lance he picked up from the mud of soil and blood. He was shouting at Kol even after the man had died, words tumbling out of his mouth as it seemed of their own accord: 'traitor', 'have me killed would you?', 'snake', 'serpent', 'laid a trap for me', 'now you die at my hands', 'revenge' … when he chanced to look up and see, through the dust and the dimming light, some thirty paces from where he stood, two riders on one horse, a great black stallion, entering into the thick of the battle.

One of the riders was a soldier in the green uniform of the Linkard battalion, the other in strangely painted dull green-and-grey armour … Gus!

So the other must be Lily.

He was sure of it, because he had, though hardly aware of it, recognized the horse first. There was no other like Maelstrom.

Lily, sitting behind Gus, was clashing swords with a Christian on her right when her leg was seized by another Christian on her left who pulled her off the horse.

Gus had just straightened from leaning far forward to run his sword clean through a red tunic. He watched the man fall back with a cry sharply cut off as blood spurted out darkly and obliterated the white cross.

Only then he saw Lily supine on the ground, and dropped down to save her from a lifted sword in the hand of a Christian by flinging his body over hers. And Maelstrom stepped over them both so they lay under his belly. Then the horse reared, neighing so loudly he could be heard above the noise of the battle. It was a terrifying sight, the huge beast neighing as his front legs climbed invisible steps of air, higher and higher, before bringing his hooves down like hammers on Christian helmets. A moment later he was standing on his front legs while his powerful back legs were kicking out, the hooves pounding into a crowd of men who were falling or leaping away.

Mordec started forward towards his friends, raising his sword still red with Kol's blood. His other hand was reaching for the battleaxe in his belt, when a Christian with a yellow plume on his helmet shot in front of him and got to the side of the horse before he could. He saw Gus and Lily rise. He saw them assailed by a new onslaught. And he saw the Christian with the yellow plume, instead of lunging at Gus or Lily when he reached them, turn, and standing beside them, thrust his sword into the red and white chest of a fellow Christian. Why would he do that?

Mordec got no nearer to the fight or the answer to his question. A crowd of green-clad boys swarmed in between him and his goal. Some seized his arms, pulling him, shouting words he could not comprehend until one word made sense to him: 'Alonso, Alonso,' they were yelling.

What did he care about Alonso when his friends were in mortal danger? He pushed through the boys—but there was no Maelstrom, no Gus or Lily to be seen, nor the Christian with the yellow plume; only the bodies of the Christian dead they and the great black horse had killed.

There was no more fighting near Mordec. The sounds of battle were not as loud. Was it possible that the battle was coming to a close? Which side then was victorious?

Judging by the heap of the dead immediately before him, Mordec would say the Christians had lost. But what of the rest of the field?

He could see no Vikings, only blue-clothed Mercians, who seemed now to outnumber the Christians. Where was the rest of the vast Christian army?

'Perhaps Gus got Lily and himself back on Maelstrom. Perhaps they escaped on him. Perhaps they're safe. That Christian helped to saved them!'

But dread filled him as fully as the berserker spirit had filled him earlier, and he felt as powerless now as he had felt powerful then. He turned to the boys in green who were still clamouring for his attention. 'Be silent!' he shouted. 'Don't yell at me. Speak so I can hear you. What are you trying to tell me?'

They saw that they had his attention at last. They spoke more quietly, but over each other, so it was still not easy to make out what they were saying. 'Alonso.' 'We know it was Alonso.'

'Alonso? You saw him? How do you know it was Alonso?'

'We saw him earlier on his horse.' 'In front of his men.' 'So we know what he looks like.' 'He's not on a horse now.' 'We can take you to him.' 'Come with us.' 'Hurry.'

'But what do you want me to do?'

'We know where he is.' 'He's hiding.' 'We know where.' 'Come on.' 'Come and get him.'

'How do you know who I am?'

'We don't know who you are but you're a Viking aren't you?'

Some grasped his arms. After looking round to make sure no enemy was about to attack him, Mordec sheathed his sword, put away his battleaxe. And after another look about him, peering through his glasses and the bars of his helmet and the gathering dimness and seeing only dark figures against a broad streak of the fiery last light of day, he went with them.

They led him in among the trees. One of them held up a flaming torch to light their way.

'Am I about to capture the leader of the Army of the Redeemed?' Mordec wondered. 'If so, what will I do with him?'

The trees were doubled by the shadows of other trees, cast by the torchlight, moving over them.

Mordec glanced back several times to make sure they were not being followed.

He could see little in the deeper dimness of the forest. He listened for sounds of battle, of clashing weapons, shouts, whinnies, hubbub; but he could hear only the groans of wounded men and the snorting of a few horses, fading behind them as they moved on.

A boy walked on either side of him, the rest streamed before him, some looking back often to make sure he was still following them.

confrontation and surrender

The boys led Mordec to the clearing on the edge of the Fenreach where Gus had taken him on Maelstrom after scooping him up to save him from an apparent attack by horsemen wielding swords.

Now Mordec was his 'Lombard self' again, in charge of his actions, and thoughtful. His thoughts were occupied with Gus and Lily. What had happened to them? How badly wounded? Were they still alive?

He did not want to admit to himself that he was almost certain they were dead. Though magnificent Maelstrom would have to be killed by any attacker first before he could get to them.

His hope that Maelstrom had saved them kept the leaden weight of sorrow at bay.

Boys whispered in his ear. '*He's* there. Go and see.'

One of them held the torch high over the bramble hedge, and Mordec stretched up to see what lay beyond the barrier. He saw someone crouching on the grass. The person was still as a rock. He was facing away from the hedge, and his head must have been bowed, because all that was visible by torchlight was a red cloak with the white cross on it, hanging to the ground from hunched shoulders.

Mordec gestured to the boys to be silent, and to the bearer of the torch to continue to hold it high, then pushed his way through the brambles, The crackle of the breaking twigs did not disturb the figure. It remained unmoving.

Mordec strode over the grass past the crouching man until he was in a position to see his face, had it not been in deep shadow. He sensed that the eyes were closed, and the hearing shut out by intense concentration. He saw the hands pressed together, held out in supplicating prayer. He saw the wooden crucifix hanging from them on a chain; the uncovered head bowed; the sword laid on the grass, its blade pointing to the praying man, its hilt with its crossguard no doubt become for him another holy cross. This was certainly Alonso.

Was he blessing his sword? Did he intend to kill himself?

Alonso was aware that he had company. But he went on with his prayer.

He was a true believer in his religion, and truly and agonizingly he now believed that he had put his soul in danger of hell.

War, he had found, was not in reality what he had envisioned it to be. He had been so sure that with Christ to guide him and great numbers of men following him, it would be a short engagement and easy victory.

He had planned to be merciful to his enemies provided they agreed to his terms.

He had taken into his vision the possibility of his own death in battle. And it had filled him with passionate joy to think that he would be dying a martyr's death and be blessed in the eyes of his Lord. A painful death was owed by Christian souls to Christ Jesus. He believed that so deeply, he had had no compunction in ordering the punishing deaths of sinners, telling himself that every pang would help to redeem their souls for all eternity. True, he had not wanted to watch the slow killings. He knew he would find the sight, and the cries of the tormented, hard to bear. He felt all things deeply. That the sufferings of men and women, and even children, must be ordered by him, he felt to be part of his Christian selflessness.

And indeed it was not the sight of bleeding men that had shocked him in the first minutes of the battle, but the unimagined sight of a horse's innards being spilled out of its slit belly that had so unexpectedly sent him flying from the field, leaning far over his horse's neck, shouting at it to go faster, faster, to the forest and in among the trees, leaving the battle and the sounds of it as far behind as he could, until he came to the bramble hedge, saw the clearing beyond, and spurred his horse into the leap of its life to get him over, as if into safety.

It was not his desertion of his soldiers that he was repenting, not the losing of the war that he was begging forgiveness for, not the souls of all those killed in battle that he was asking mercy for, but the weakness of his own spirit when he had so suddenly understood that he too could be cut open, and that he could not after all endure a martyr's death, could not take up his cross and follow Jesus Christ who had died for him, could not endure agony. Could not now, never could. He had been wrong to believe that God had chosen *him* to bring the English into the redemption that the Roman Church alone could grant them.

Mordec stood before the kneeling, praying Abbot Alonso de Llama. He planted his feet well apart, hooked his thumbs in his belt, on either side his battleaxe and dagger. His stained sword hung at his side. He knew he was formidable figure in his armour and the strange iron helmet.

'Alon-so!' he intoned in as deep a voice as he could. 'Look up, Alon-so!'

The kneeling man looked up, tipping back his tonsured head. Mordec remembered rather than distinctly saw the pink scalp, the circle of yellow curls.

What Alonso saw in the flickering red light was a figure of iron with the face of a beaked devil.

He did not rise. He pressed the wooden crucifix to his soft red lips, then held it out towards the apparition from hell.

'Keep away from me, Satan!' he cried out in a trembling voice. 'I have confessed my sins to Christ. You cannot take my soul!'

Mordec laughed, harshly and mirthlessly.

'What would I want with your soul, Abbot Alonso de Llama? I want nothing of you except your surrender. It is you who wanted me. Remember? "Most wanted, Mordec son of Hauk". *I am Mordec son of Hauk.* Now, what do you want me for?'

Slowly the Abbot rose to his feet. Keeping his attention on Mordec, he reached for his sword tentatively, expecting Mordec to stop him taking hold of it. Mordec did not move.

Alonso snatched up his sword and held it on his shoulder. His long cloak was open in front, and Mordec saw a dagger in his belt. He was ready to seize his own weapons if he needed to, but he doubted the Abbot would attack him. There was something too abject about the man.

The Abbot did not advance on Mordec. He edged sideways, slowly, towards the horse grazing on the bank of the stream.

Mordec's hands had not moved. He laughed again, softly this time, and with more real amusement.

'Want to escape?' he said. 'Run away? Again? You? Alonso de Llama, the Pope's warlord? You who would conquer England! You have found out that all you can do is flee? And you think I will let you?'

Alonso dropped his sword and fell again to his knees. His hands came together again, not this time in prayer to his god but to his captor.

He spoke huskily. 'I do not plead for my life,' he said. 'I plead only that you kill me quickly.'

'You fear pain, do you?' Mordec scoffed. 'You, who inflicted it on so many?'

In this angle of the torchlight, Mordec could see that beads of sweat decorated Alonso's brow. His cheeks were stained with tears he had shed.

'I have prayed. I have confessed. I have hope of heaven. You may kill me now.'

'I will not ask for your permission when I decide to kill you,' Mordec said. 'What matters now is what *I* want from *you.*'

He paused. Alonso did not move.

'What I want from you, Abbot Alonso de Llama, is *surrender.*'

He cried out this last word into the night. It was greeted by a shout of approval from beyond the hedge. The torch-bearer waved his torch up and down by way of applause.

'Get up!' Mordec commanded. 'Pick up your sword. Lay it across the palms of your hands, and bring it to me.'

Obediently, stumbling for a moment as his foot trod on the edge of his cloak, Alonso did as he was told.

'Kneel on one knee.' Mordec commanded.

The Abbot knelt.

'Now hand me your sword and say loudly "I surrender".'

Alonso glared at the iron mask of his conqueror.

Mordec, looking through his glasses and through the helmet's windows with their iron frames, thought that never before had he seen a look of such hatred as he saw now, clearly, even in this poor light, in the cold eyes of his mortal foe. And it was not hatred mixed with anger; it was hatred in a torment of despair.

Alonso, kneeling on one knee, holding up the sword athwart his palms towards Mordec, groaned through clenched teeth, 'I surrender.'

'Louder!'

'I surrender!' Alonso piped shrilly, and sobbed and hung his head. The boys cheered.

Mordec took the sword and shouted for the boys to come to him. They pressed through the brambles, the torchlight swinging wildly.

'Alonso has surrendered,' Mordec announced as if to a much larger crowd. 'The Army of the Redeemed is defeated.'

The boys cheered again.

One of them called out, 'England is saved.'

'I'm not sure about that,' Mordec said pleasantly. 'You still have us Vikings to contend with.'

At which all the boys, being too young to know when a man was being serious, laughed.

They tied their captive's wrists together with a bow-string. One took away his dagger. Two boys, giggling, shared his cloak, letting it trail behind them.

Mordec handed over Alonso's sword, and his own sword, battleaxe, and dagger for some of them to carry. 'I know better than to enter the Fenreach or the Earldom of Linkard bearing arms.'

He lifted off his helmet. The boys took it and put it on Alonso. They lifted the Abbot on to his horse, and seated him facing the tail.

The Abbot said nothing, made no resistance.

They led the horse, with its iron-masked rider looking backwards, to the Fenreach, across its meadows and on to those of Linkard. The torch burned down to a glow of its pitch, and they walked on by starlight.

They were met by soldiers with yellow plumes, red plumes and blue plumes in their helmets, some on foot and some mounted, who cheered when they heard who the prisoner was. One of the yellow feathers rode ahead as fast as he could in the dark to take the news to Linkard Castle. The rest joined the marchers as an escort, so it was quite a long procession that arrived at the drawbridge.

Still mounted back to front, the Abbot was led into the castle, which was lighted by many flaming torches on the walls and in the hands of servants. In the inner courtyard he was pulled off his horse.

A red feather solder and a blue feather soldier stepped forward together to seize him.

'Hold!' Mordec shouted. Then more quietly but very firmly he said, 'This man is my prisoner. I will take him to the Earl.'

The men stood aside as Mordec gripped the Abbot's shoulder.

'Lead the way,' Mordec commanded, and they did. The boys followed Mordec and his prisoner, carrying Mordec's arms and Alonso's ceded sword.

The Earl of Linkard received them wearing his green army uniform and a narrow iron coronet.

Queen Bertha stood on one side of him in a gown of black silk and a silver crown, and Sir Baz stood on the other in his armour, its whiteness nobly soiled by the stains of battle. His hands were bandaged.

Father Donlock sat at the table in his church vestments, ready with pen and paper to record what would clearly be a ceremony. He did not rise as Mordec and the Abbot entered, but keeping his head bent looked up at them from under his eyebrows.

One of the boys, bearing the Abbot's sword on his cupped hands, came forward and laid it carefully, ceremoniously, on the table before the Earl.

Mordec took the helmet off the Abbot's head and tucked it under his arm.

Alonso stood looking straight ahead, his eyes hooded, almost closed.

'Abbot Alonso de Llama,' the Earl said stiffly, standing stiffly, 'I am Reginald Earl of Linkard. I am one of the Commanders of the English forces who have lately engaged your invading army. Beside me is Queen Bertha of the Fenreach whose soldiers were also among the English forces. And this is Sir Baz, who commanded our archers. I take it this sword that lies before me is your sword, given up in surrender. Do you have something to say to me?'

The Abbot opened his eyes wide and turned them on Father Donlock.

'I would ask your priest,' he growled, 'if he has sent an explanation to the Holy Father in Rome for his treachery.'

Father Donlock did not meet the glare of the cold blue eyes. He kept his head down and busied himself with writing what the Abbot had said.

Mordec spoke.

'Yes,' he said. 'Yes, illustrious lord, this man is Abbot Alonso de Llama, leader of the invading Army of the Redeemed. He has presented me, Mordec son of Hauk, soldier of the Viking army, with his sword and declared his surrender. He is my prisoner. A prisoner of the Vikings. His sword is my booty. I request that you, illustrious lord, Earl Reginald of Linkard, and you, illustrious lady, Queen Bertha of the Fenreach, hold my prisoner in custody until Commander Tostig of the Viking army sends for him.'

The Earl and Queen Bertha were silent. They had expected the Abbot to surrender formally to them.

'Though as I see it, we will be acting as proxies for King Aelfrid,' the Earl had said to the Queen. 'We cannot claim that ours was the major force that won this war.'

Queen Bertha had agreed.

They acknowledged without rancour rthe King of Mercia's higher right, but here was this Viking—one they both knew well, and had always thought of as a pleasant well-behaved lad as far as Vikings could be pleasant and well-behaved—arrogantly claiming that the leader of the defeated army had surrendered to him, which was as much as to say that the victory belonged to his army, his people.

And though the Vikings were allies at present (even indispensable allies, the Earl would have admitted if pressed), they were invaders themselves in English eyes.

'He wanted to bargain with me for his life.' Mordec went on. 'And not only for his life, but also for his comfort. He fears torture.'

'What did you tell him? Did you make him any promises?'

'No. Commander Tostig will decide his punishment. For the present, I ask you not to take his life. What else you do to him is your decision.'

On hearing the word 'torture', the Abbot had gasped, opened his mouth to speak—but said nothing, gulped, and drooped his head again.

'But,' Mirdec went on, insistently, 'we want him alive to agree to the terms we will demand.'

'If we hold him prisoner for you, we too must have a say in the terms of his surrender,' the Earl declared firmly.

'You have earned that right. We will respect it. King Aelfrid too will make his demands. But the Abbot is first and foremost our captive.'

The heart of Father Donlock melted for the forlorn figure of Alonso, though he knew the Abbot's reputation, and had long believed his deeds were a stain on the Church and a blasphemy against the gospels. Unable to say a word of comfort to the abject broken man, his sympathy with wretchedness expressed itself in a rebuke to Mordec.

'*Your* captive? Did not our boys find him first?'

'Found him, yes. But it was to me that he surrendered.'

He turned back to the Earl.

'So I ask you, illustrious lord, will you hold him for my Commander? May I suggest in your prison tower (which I remember all too well), under close guard until we can come for him? And there's another thing I must ask of you—special dispensation for our men to come armed on to your land when they come to fetch him away.'

The Earl and the Queen turned away to face the high window and the faint light of dawn.

'If Aelfrid insists on a formal surrender to him personally, he can take up the matter with the Vikings,' the Earl whispered. 'I think I can consent to what Mordec is asking.'

The Queen nodded. She said loudly, 'Very well. But I still think it's a pity we can't do what we like with him. My lioness would be pleased to play with him.'

They turned back and the Queen was delighted to see terror on the Abbot's fair face.

'Your request,' the Earl told Mordec, 'that we hold this man prisoner until he can be handed over to Viking guards is granted. And they have permission to be armed on that one day. They will be escorted by my own armed guards.'

The boys bound the Abbot's legs so that he could barely hobble, and tied the reins of his horse round his waist by which to lead him like a beast to the prison tower.

They danced about him as they drew him away.

For them this war had been a jolly adventure, and not only was it still going on, it was getting better every moment.

Father Donlock took up his pen and paper and left the room.

The ceremony, such as it had been, that ended the war, was over.

The Earl kissed the Queen's hand, clapped Mordec on the shoulder, and went to bed.

'I have had no news of Lily,' Bertha said to Mordec. 'Do you know where she is? Is she … living?'

'I saw her,' Mordec replied. 'She was with Gus. They were both riding Maelstrom.'

'Taking part in the battle?'

'Yes.'

'Did it seem to you that they were winning?'

'I couldn't tell. I only saw them for a moment before the boys called me away to follow the Abbot. Maelstrom himself is a mighty weapon.'

He was not sure if he was shirking a description of what he had really seen in order to spare Queen Bertha or himself.

The Queen embraced him and held him for a few moments, as though to absorb some of the strength of his youth, or to give him some of the strength of her pride.

Looking for one man in particular, Father Donlock hurried through the rooms of the palace, breaking the news of the invader's surrender to everyone he came across. He announced that the war was over and had ended in 'victory for the English and the Vikings' to the soldiers waiting in the courtyard, the guards of the night watch, women sweeping the kitchen floor, and the doctors tending the injured in the spacious courthouse-turned-hospital. And there it was he found the man he had been urgently seeking: Mel de Gustybuss, acting as nurse to the wounded.

As soon as he had heard and digested the good news, Mel postponed demanding the details of the surrender that Father Donlock was yet to give him, and hurried to his pigeons. Soon there were birds flying through the bright morning to the Troll in his buried mansion—who would send the messages on by dwarf to Trygghaven.

Adam the Lombard at Guardia Brevis in Italy had exchanged carrier pigeons with Julius chiefly in order to receive news of the war in which his grandson and his daughter's husband were fighting. So Julius sent a message of victory, including mention of Mordec's role as receiver of the Abbot's surrender, flying to him.

When Adam had read the good news he wrote a letter which he sent—feeling a deep sense of relief, and a triumph that crowed like a rooster in the privacy of his head—with a strong rider on a swift steed to the Pope in Rome. He warned the messenger to guard his life and leave the moment he had handed over the letter to the Pope's guards, such bad news for that potentate did the letter contain.

Queen Bertha lent Mordec a horse from her stable—Roman Ruin, the very one Gus had been lent by Lily to race against her on the Roman road when she had been riding Maelstrom; and the very one on which he had once galloped to save Mordec from execution.

Mordec was escorted to the northern boundary of Linkard by Sir Baz.

They rode side by side in their armour, the wounded knight and the Viking in the fearsome helmet. Wounded though he was, the knight rode sitting up straight on his white horse, which was unhurt.

Baz explained to Mordec that he had dismounted after the young archers he'd commanded had emptied their quivers, and had sent them and the horse back to the Fenreach. Only then had he himself entered the fight.

When they were through the guarded gate, Sir Baz handed over Mordec's own weapons to him, and the Abbot's sword. They parted with promises to meet again, for they were not only allies, but old friends.

ambush and a vision

In the great Battle of Mercia, fought on the northern fields of the kingdom, the Pope's Army of the Redeemed was heavily defeated by the combined forces of King Aelfrid and the Vikings. About half the number of Christian soldiers who marched to war wearing the white cross on the red ground were slain or too badly wounded to join in the retreat. Their dead were left to the vultures, the wolves, and the maggots; their wounded to live or die—and if they lived, to find their own way to safety. It is not known how many of their gravely injured, if any at all, survived after the retreat of the remnant of the Christian army.

Neither the Mercians nor the Vikings took prisoners. When the new day dawned, the Mercians gathered up their own dead for burial, and carried their wounded to Tamworth, there to die or be found by their kin and taken home.

The Vikings buried some of their dead—not more than one hundred—in a burrow near the monastery of Barleyfield, and some, the few captains and heroes who had fallen, they sent at dawn in burning ships to Valhalla. The wounded were lain in the their tents and tended by the wives and daughters of the Viking farmers of Northumbria. For many of them these were their own wives and daughters, but those who had sailed from the north were as tenderly cared for.

A spirit of triumph in victory prevailed among the Vikings and was often said in saga and song to have healed wounds by its own strength and even to have raised some of the dead!

The Christian soldiers who survived were still numerous. With no leader, no orders to fight on or to retreat, they retreated.

They did not march away in unison, but straggled singly or in groups, some who were lame but strong enough to move helped by their comrades. They made slow progress, and weariness, hunger, pain and loss of blood took a heavy toll of the company as the weak gave up the struggle.

The captains of the Mercian army lusted to follow them and cut them down, but King Aelfrid said it would be 'unchristian' and to let them go in peace.

'Besides,' said the King, seated in state beside his Queen, 'the forces of Cornwall will meet them and have yet to satisfy the thirst of their swords.'

'The thirst of their swords,' said the Queen.

In truth, however 'unchristian' a late attack on the retreating remnant of Alonso's army might be, King Aelfrid was hoping for it. He wished that the Pope's invaders would be wholly wiped out, leaving none foolish enough to plot revenge.

He knew why the Cornish army had not attacked the rear of the Christian force on the day of the battle; that their king had been captured and killed by a Viking who had not heard of the alliance agreed between the English, the Cornish, and the Vikings.

And he knew also that the Cornishmen were awaiting the arrival of the Earl of Felldown to lead them against the Christians.

'Felldown's troops will ambush the rest of the invaders in their bases,' he told his Council with confidence.

But Earl Botham of Felldown, his daughter Captain Anwid, and their small force of guards and girl warriors were still far from the border of Cornwall.

On the day of the battle they were nearing the southern coast, intending to make better speed on the well-worn road along the shore.

As they camped in a small dense forest of big-boled trees on the very night when, unbeknown to them, their allies had won the great battle that ended the war, they were quiet as they munched their bread and drank from their flagons, thinking of the long march ahead, and the longer one yet to come when they would lead the troops of Cornwall to fight the Army of the Redeemed.

None of them were excited by the prospect. They were in sombre mood.

'Listen, Dellibeth,' Captain Anwid said softly to the girl beside her. 'If both the Earl and I should die in battle, go to Cogg Hall and live there, and look after our land and our tenants. It will be yours. I left a paper with Earl Reginald of Linkard signed by my father and me, and witnessed by Donlock the priest. It says that we bequeath Felldown to you.'

Dellibeth was more concerned about the possible death of her Captain than she was with the benefit she might gain from it.

'Oh, but you must not die, Captain. Don't speak of it. I don't want to hear of it. We must sleep now.'

And Dellibeth rolled herself up in her seagreen cloak, covering herself from head to toe, and did not hear the Captain telling her softly that if she too should die in this war, Felldown would go to the Kings of Mercia 'who one day will unify the whole country under their crown'.

Next day as they were riding through the forest, Captain Anwid suddenly threw back her head and called out joyfully, 'I can smell it! I can smell the sea! We are nearly there.'

It had always been the sweetest scent to her.

Her last word was almost drowned out by the shouting of many voices, and from behind the trees armed men came running, their breasts bearing the white crosses on a red ground that marked them as soldiers of the Pope's army.

Surrounded by upraised swords, the Earl, his guards, Anwid and her girls overcame their surprise in a moment, had their own weapons out, and rode furiously into their attackers on all sides.

Their horses were soon disabled, and they fought on the ground. They were so greatly outnumbered that they knew, every one of them, that there was little hope of survival, let alone of victory. But they fought long and valiantly.

Anwid, though fiercely engaged herself, saw her father standing for a moment between two fallen Christians, and then go down himself under an onslaught of many swords.

His guards were soon dispatched, though every one of them fought on despite wounds—some even when they were on their knees—until they could no longer hold their weapons.

The girl warriors were just as brave and persistent, being proud of their skill and endurance and unafraid in the face of certain death.

The Christian soldiers, given pause at first for a moment or two by the sight of young girls fighting like men, nevertheless set upon them without mercy.

When the Christians saw all the English lying still, some upon others, some with their faces in the mashed leaves of the forest floor, some on their backs with their eyes wide open, none of them moving, they went off shouting and laughing, carrying their few dead, proud that they had done their part so well in this war of conquest.

Two of the English party were still alive.

One, hardly hurt herself, though having wounded three, was tall red-headed Dellibeth, the natural leader of the girl warriors.

She eased herself out from under the neck of a dead horse and the legs of a Felldown guard, stood and looked about her at the carnage. Tears coursed down her face, though she restrained her sobs.

She picked her way among the corpses, seeking her shipmates. She found all of them, and all were dead. She laid them gently on their backs, crossed their arms on their breasts over their swords, and closed their eyes. She kissed each of them on the lips. Her tears fell faster and she sobbed aloud.

She came to the body of Earl Botham, removed his helmet and arranged his arms as she had those of her companions. She folded her tattered sea-green cloak and placed it as a pillow under his head, and kissed his brow.

She searched on. 'Where are you, my captain,' she murmured, lifting the bodies of the Felldown guards with respectful care. But Captain Anwid was not beneath them. Not under the carcass of a horse. Not lying alone half-buried in the leaves.

'Captain!' she called aloud at last.

And she was answered by a faint groan. Dellibeth ran towards the sound, and found the captain leaning against a tree, her hand on a wound in her side, blood seeping through her fingers.

'Captain! Oh Captain!'

'Help me, Dellibeth … I must get … to the sea!' The words were barely breathed.

Dellibeth understood. She put an arm round Anwid's waist, and bore almost all her weight as they slowly moved towards the light beyond the forest. The Captain's head rested on her shoulder as the wounded woman put her feet, loose as those of a puppet, one before the other, believing that she was walking.

The trees thinned, the light grew, and then they were standing in an enormous whiteness, and a vast glitter lay spread before them stretching to the edge of the world.

'It is … the sea!' the Captain moaned. 'On … on …'

And on they went. And soon they were on sand. Dellibeth now lifted her Captain in her arms, carried her like a baby and trudged over the hampering sand towards the breaking surf.

Anwid could feel the light on her eyes but she could not see through it. The light itself was mostly a mist, except for that glitter which she knew was the sea.

Then over the glitter and through the mist that lay upon it, a shape emerged. She stretched an arm towards it, trying to speak but only hoarsely groaning, 'Look! … Look … there! It is … she … it is she.'

'Who is it, my dear?' Dellibeth asked, her salt tears entering her mouth as she spoke. 'Who?'

'The … Good … Ship … Good. She … has come … for … me.'

Dellibeth stopped at the foamy edge of a wave's reach.

'Carry … me … onto her. … please … please …'

Dellibeth waded into the water.

'Yes … yes … on … on.'

Dellibeth waded deeper. It reached her knees. She lifted her burden higher. The water reached her chest and the salt sea entered the Captain's wound.

She cried out—but with words, and they sounded not pained but contented: 'Home … I … am … home.'

Her head fell back, Dellibeth saw that she was smiling, and then felt by her weight that she was dead.

Dellibeth did not stop walking on the floor of the sea. Her head was still above the waves, though the next one would wash over it. She went on until her dear burden was quite submerged. Still she did not let go of her, but clutching her close, she took a deep breath, and—keeping her eyes open though the salt stung them—swam under water with the strokes of one arm towards a cluster of rocks.

She pressed the body of her Captain between two of them, down, down, until it was tightly wedged, held fast—a gift to the sea of herself as the Captain would have wished.

the prisoner in the tower

Abbot Alonso sat in the prison tower of Linkard, or knelt in prayer on its hard floor plastered with bird droppings, in deep mourning for his lost soul.

He expected that one day soon he would be fetched by Vikings to some sort of trial.

He did not trust the word of Mordec son of Hauk that he would not be tortured. He knew he should be praying for a martyr's death so he could do penance for his desertion of the battlefield and the breaking of his vows that he would bring all the Western Isles into the fold of the Church or die in the attempt. Instead, he had fled in terror. And even now what he prayed for was to be spared pain.

On the second day of his imprisonment, Mel de Gustybuss came to see him. He was admitted by a red-feather guard.

The guard said, 'I'll lock the door while you're with him. But I'll be just outside the door. If he gives you any trouble, shout and I'll be with you in a flash.'

Give trouble? The man was on his knees, his pink pate with its circle of fair curls bowed over his clasped hands.

'Good-day to you, Abbot,' Mel de Gustybuss said cheerily.

He had asked Father Donlock what he should call the Abbot. Father? Brother?

'Just Abbot will do,' Father Donlock had replied, looking as though he could have made other suggestions that wouldn't have been seemly. 'That's what I called him when I visited him yesterday.'

Father Donlock had heard the Abbot's confession. It was long, it was a history of horrors, and it had chilled the good father to the bone.

'I always meant to be fair—and truthful,' the Abbot had said pleadingly. 'I was fair to the wicked Sam of the West when we had our silent debate. I could have said that he had lost, but I knew that he had won. So I could not prove his wickedness. I only condemned those to punishment who had been proved guilty of heresy. I could never witness their punishment. I told myself it was to keep myself from gloating over the well-deserved suffering of heretics. But it wasn't. I was deceiving myself. The truth is that … that … I am a coward, a worm, who broke his vows to God.'

He had risen suddenly to his feet, had shrunk against the stone wall, put up both hands and cried out, 'No more, no more. I have not yet fully confessed. There is more. There is worse. Do not give me absolution. Not yet. Go away, Father.'

'Do you want me to return to hear the rest?'

'Yes, yes. Before they take me away. But I have not told you all yet. I will, I will.'

'And this man,' Father Donlock had thought, as he descended the winding stairs and walked back briskly to the castle, 'wanted to be the ruler of England and all the isles. The good Lord has spared us a fearful fate!'

In Father Donlock's mind, it was his god that had saved them, not the Mercian army or the Vikings. Armies were the instruments of God, and without God they decided nothing. 'Except the Lord win the battle, they labour in vain who fight it,' he had said to himself.

Now the prisoner, standing head down, shoulders bent, at the window, looking out over the bog of Ballylee, did not return Mel's greeting.

Mel was not put out in the least by his forbidding silence. He took off his eyeglasses, polished them vigorously with a silk handkerchief plucked from a pocket in his short, well-tailored grey coat, replaced them on his nose, and continued.

'Thing is, Abbot, your clothes are torn and stained. The Earl asks if you want to appear in them before King Aelfrid and the Viking high command for the ceremony of surrender and presentation of the terms. It's a choice I could understand. If that's what you decide, end of discussion. No pressure. But if you feel you should appear in garb suitable to your high office as Abbot and leader of the Army of the Redeemed, say the word and Mel de Gustybuss is at your service. Oh, by the way, that's my name. I should have said. Should have properly introduced myself. Mel de Gustybuss, Art Director to Reginald, Earl of Linkard.'

'I should be in a garment of repentance,' the Abbot wailed quietly. 'Sackcloth and ashes.'

'Good choice, I happen to have a nice piece of sackcloth. Came wrapped round a bale of leather leggings in quite the wrong colour. The Earl had stipulated green for his soldiers. The guards are normally divided according to rank. The more experienced wear red feathers, new recruits blue feathers, and yellow feathers are for the officers. But for active duty, the Earl and I reckoned green uniforms for all. Well, as I was saying, these leggings were dyed red. We had to try and re-dye them ourselves. The effort was not a success. They came out brown. But that's beside the present point. What I was meaning to say was, the sackcloth may be the very thing for you. What do you think?'

'A garment of repentance,' Alonso repeated.

'As for the ashes part,' Mel went on, his ever-inventive imagination hard at work, 'no problem there. The kitchen is never out of them. You'll point out to me the places where you want them rubbed in, and I'll do the rest. I see you have a wooden cross. How would it be if we put a narrow but suitably rough rope round your middle, and you could hang the cross from it? I'd lose the gold chain if I were you. String would match the outfit better. Now if you will permit me, I'll just need your shoulder-width, arm length, and nape-to knee …'

He drew a measuring tape from around his neck.

But Alonso held out both hands to keep Mel away.

'No?' Mel said. 'You'd rather I didn't? Well, I've seen you now, and as it will be a loose garment anyway, I think I'll get it about right. In any case a garment of repentance should not be a good fit, wouldn't you agree?'

'A black hood,' Alonso said.

'Right! Why not? A black hood. How do you want it? Outlining the face, 'Mel gestured to show what he meant, 'or coming far forward? Maybe a generous-sized cowl that can be folded back on the shoulders like a shawl? I can do it in wool, and black dye is easy. No? Very well, a hood it will be. And how about a cloak?'

'No.'

'Nothing else, then. Well, I'll get going with the order right away. Enjoy the rest of your day, Abbot.'

He knocked on the door and the guard let him out. On the stairs he passed Larry the Executioner coming up.

'Larry? Will your services be needed? I was given to understand that the Vikings …'

'The Vikings will have the final say whether he lives or dies, yes, that is correct,' Larry said. 'I'm just paying a visit out of curiosity. Want to get a look at the man. I was reckoned to be too old to fight, so I never saw him riding ahead of his troops. They say he cut quite a grand figure.'

'Not now he doesn't,' Mel said. 'Abject, abject, That's what he is. All he wants is a garment of repent-ance. I'm off to see to it. But wait a moment—will they let you in? I'm told he's not allowed visitors. I only got to him because the Earl wants him to look right at the surrender. Or at least, I suggested to the Earl that he might want that. And now—he won't even have a cloak. The prisoner, I mean.'

'It comes written,' Larry said, 'that I, as the Earl's honourable executioner—that's what it says, "honourable executioner"—shall have free access to the prisoners.'

'You won't find him chatty,' Mel warned.

'He should be crying all day and begging for mercy.' Larry said. 'I've heard all kinds of beggings for mercy.'

'He won't do that either,' Mel said.

But he was wrong. No sooner had Larry introduced himself as 'the Earl's honourable executioner', than Alonso fell on his knees before him and pleaded for mercy.

'*You're* not to be executed,' Larry said. 'Leastways, not here. The Vikings will come for you. They do the job differently. We garotte you first, then drop you in the Bog of Ballylee, that dark wet stretch you can see over there. Had two customers last month. One Bill Hitchem who used to be the Court defender. And the other—would you believe it?—was a woman. Until she came along, there hadn't been any women for me to execute. But these two, you see, had been treating the bondsmen in the Bond House house real bad. Eating the food the Lady Jessica—that's the Earl's daughter—ordered for the men and boys. She found out what was going on, Lady Jessica did, when the Earl said the men and older boys must be trained for the war. They told their trainer what they'd had to endure at the hands of this Master Hitchem and Mistress Pillikin, and he told Lady Jessica. Deprived of food, overworked, knocked about ... Oh, was she upset about it! She ordered a full trial for mutiny, and Father Donlock acted as defender, and all he could do was ask for mercy for them, because their wickedness was proved over and over again by many witnesses, and the pair of them, Bill and Coo they called each other, were sentenced to death. A very neat job of their execution I did, both times, though I say so myself. I've invented a chair that tips them neatly … But to come to the point. The Vikings do it differently. They go to much greater lengths as you know, of course. Make a real job of it, they do. Aren't after neatness, or speed. They take off your limbs, and your head, then they split you open from here to here, fold back your ribs this way and that … What's wrong? Abbot? Have you fainted or something?'

Alonso *had* fainted. Larry called in the guard, who lifted the unconscious man into a chair and casually slapped his face this way and that a few times, until the man's eyes opened.

'Give him some water,' the guard said. 'He'll be alright. Look he's opened his eyes. He's beginning to stir.'

'So he is,' Larry agreed. 'Stirring at last—as the stew said to the ladle.'

the round table

The prisoner of war, Abbot Alonso de Llama, was fetched one morning from the tower of Linkard by three mounted Vikings, three mounted Mercians, a cart driven by an official of the Mercian king's stables, and Crispin Cuthburd who had come—without King Aelfrid's orders, but with Queen Aethelwynne's admiration—to see that the diplomatic protocols were properly observed.

Crispin Cuthburd was escorted up the winding stairs by the two Linkardian officers who were to hand over custody of the Abbot. When the diplomat saw how the prisoner, the leader of the Pope's defeated army, was dressed, he raised both hands and declared it would not do.

But Larry the Executioner was there, waiting with Alonso, and he explained that the clothing was exactly what the Abbot himself had asked for: his feet in sandals, his body in the ash-coloured—and carefully ash-stained—monk's habit that Mel de Gustybuss had designed for him, with a thin rough rope sound his waist, from which his wooden crucifix depended on a string.

His head was covered with a black hood that came far forward, concealing his face from all but those

221

who might peer inside it—which only Larry the executioner did when he'd helped settle the prisoner in the cart, on the bare boards (another point of diplomatic objection).

When Cuthburd said that 'the representative of the Pope should at least have a cushion', the Vikings laughed.

'Farewell, bad monk,' Larry said, reaching over the side of the cart to pat the tied hands. 'The road is rough, the bones will be shaken, but your dinner waits at the end of it—as the winding-sheet said to the worm.'

Alonso was so knocked about in the cart that by the time he reached the palace of Tamworth he was judged by Crispin Cuthburd to be in need of two days rest in a grand palace chamber before he would be fit to parley with the King. The Viking guards insisted that the talks start the next day. The Earl of Linkard and Queen Bertha were due to arrive then, as well as Commander Tostig with his party.

Crispin Cuthburd sat in the middle of the chamber where Alonso was lodged with a Viking and a palace guard.

He addressed the abject figure curled up on his side on the enormous bed dressed with spreads and curtains of fine stuffs from India and Damascus, with his sandals off, but the hood totally concealing his face.

'I am a poet. I cannot say that I am a pious man. But I was baptized and I appweciate the rich poetry of holy scwipture. I plan to write an epic poem about the war. If you would care to tell me your thoughts about it, I can pwomise to incorporate them in my poem—though I might take a little poetic license when it comes to fitting them into my chosen metwical pattern. Please feel free to speak. I am all ears.'

Alonso put his hands together, clasping the wooden crucifix between them, and said not a word to the listener. After a while the disappointed poet got up and went away.

The Abbot did not sleep much, did not eat much.

He wouldn't lower himself further to beg not to be put in the hands of the Vikings, he resolved.

He dozed for a while, woke, and resolved that he would lower himself as far down as he could go begging not to be put in the hands of the Vikings.

The Viking party that arrived for the conference consisted of three persons: Commander Tostig, Harold Goldmountain, and Mordec.

They had no sooner arrived, greeted by three notes on a trumpet at the open door of the throne room where the royal council sat—half the old men to the left of the thrones and half to the right—than the trumpet sounded again for the arrival of the Earl of Linkard with Father Donlock, and Queen Bertha with Sir Baz clothed as always in white. The Earl now wore a golden coronet, and Queen Bertha, dressed in silver silk that seemed to pour down from her shoulders like a moonlit river, had crowned herself with a circlet of silver fronted by a large diamond. She seemed to be a source of light for the whole room.

A third fanfare announced the entrance of King Aelfrid and Queen Aethelwynne in robes of damson silk and ermine.

The councillors rose. Queen Aethelwynne and Queen Bertha embraced, while the councillors, Earl Reginald, Father Donlock, and Sir Baz bowed low. The Vikings stood straight and still.

When the ceremony of greeting was over, Mordec presented himself to Queen Bertha, and asked her to walk with him in the grand passages of Tamworth palace.

'Queen Bertha,' he said, 'is Lily safe?'

'She is.'

'And Gus?'

'He was wounded before the great battle.'

'Who wounded him? How?'

'Lily did. She nearly killed him.'

'Please tell me how that came to be.'

'They met in the forest. Lily went to find her horse and the thief who had stolen him. A stranger appeared, riding on him, in full armour and a helmet that concealed his face—like Lily's own. She was ready for a fight—she could not know that it was Gus.'

'And Gus could not know that the warrior who confronted him was Lily.'

'So they fought.'

'And Lily won! Against Gus!'

'As he lay bleeding, choking to death on his own blood—as she was about to strike the final blow—he managed to speak one word that stopped her.'

'One word? What was it? Gus would not ask for mercy.'

'Your name.'

'*My* name? Odds-bods! I saved Gus's life yet again?'

'Why are you smiling?' Queen Bertha asked.

'Am I smiling? Well, I'm sorry of course that Gus was hurt. I'm glad he survived. I smile only because Gus is a warrior born, yet Lily won their battle to the death.'

'Lily too is a warrior born—and it's plain now that she's the better one. Gus recovered from his wound enough to fight in the great battle. They went into it together, both of them mounted on Maelstrom. They tell a strange story—how they were both helped to win against great odds by a Christian soldier.'

'Yes. And by Maelstrom,' Mordec said. 'By a Christian soldier *and* by the horse.'

'How do you know?'

'I was there. I saw what happened. Gus flung himself over Lily as she lay on the ground—pulled from the horse by an enemy soldier. Maelstrom stepped over them to protect them. It was wonderful to see. Maelstrom killed many with the powerful weapons of his hooves. The Christians scattered, then came back, thick upon them. The last I saw was one of the Christian soldiers using his sword against his own side, helping to keep them from Gus and Lily. So they were not mortally hurt?'

'They were not.'

'Nor Maelstrom?'

'Nor Maelstrom. But tell me, Mordec son of Hauk who knows so much, do you know why a Christian soldier would risk his own life to save them?'

Mordec shook his head. He had no answer. He despised treachery, but this was treachery that aided his friends.

'I fear they'll marry,' Queen Bertha said.

'You are against it?'

'He's a Viking. I am thankful that you Vikings helped us to defeat Alonso's army, but you are not to be trusted. I made the mistake of trusting a Viking once. Then my daughter stooped to marry one of you, Now my granddaughter is about to lower herself in the same way. But at least they will be living with me and not at the other end of the world. Shall I take a word from you to Gus?'

'Yes, please, illustrious lady. I'd like Gus and Lily to know that I saw what happened to them in the battle. And tell Gus that I will get word to his father Hakon and his mother Tove that—'

'That he fought, and fought bravely?'

'That he fought, and fought bravely. It is the truth. I'll tell them what I saw and they'll believe me. It will count with them that I am the one saying it.'

***

King Aelfrid had ordered his carpenter to make a large round table, not for this particular conference, nor for his regular meetings with his Council, but because he had had a dream that the table would become the most famous table in the world when a king and his knights would sit round it of whom great stories would be told down through the ages.

The table had been made, and placed in a quiet room with only one door, opening not into the palace but onto a courtyard. It had been there for nearly a year, but had not been put to use until now. (It

226

was the very same Round Table that was to become famous in the reign of King Arthur, which started more than a hundred years from that day.)

In the afternoon, the door was shut and locked and six guards stood stiffly outside it.

Candelabra fixed to the wood-panelled walls had been lighted inside the room.

Twelve of thirteen chairs were occupied: three by the Vikings; two by Queen Bertha and Sir Baz; two by Earl Reginald and Father Donlock; two by the king and Queen of Mercia; two on either side of them by men of law; and one, across from the King, by Abbot Alonso de Llama.

The empty place was where the Duke of Bassington would have sat, but he had been killed by a mass onslaught of the enemy near the end of the great battle, in which—King Aelfrid proudly told his allies—the Duke had bravely and skilfully led the Mercian army to victory. There would be monuments raised to him, the King said, and Mercia's debt to him would never be forgotten.

Then the King turned to present concerns.

The Abbot's hands were not bound. He wore his garment of repentance, but his head was bare, his face plain to see. All who had not seen him close up before were surprised how young the Abbot looked, and that even with the signs of fear and grief on his face it was a pretty sight, like the face of a girl, with the cherry-red lips, the yellow curls (more of them on the pink pate since the tonsure had not been attended to with a razor), and the violet-blue eyes fringed with long thick eyelashes.

The same thought was in the minds of several of the victors who sat there staring at him for a few moments: 'This was the man who has terrified multitudes?'

As soon as he was seated, the Abbot's eyes had sought for Mordec, from whose expression he thought he might gauge the mood of his judges. The only impression he got was that Mordec, peering back at him over his glasses, was slightly amused to see him here.

Next the prisoner looked at Commander Tostig, who frowned at him, so he shifted his gaze quickly to the last of the three Vikings, Harald Goldmountain, dressed finely in white and purple. He was not looking at the prisoner. And his expression was not angry. He might be merciful.

Father Donlock gave him a slight nod and turned his head away.

The Earl did not look at him. But the handsome and despondent Sir Baz met his gaze impassively.

It was with some relief Alonso rested his eyes on Queen Bertha and her silvery beauty, although she glared at him; but after a few moments the diamond in her crown brought the word 'vanity' to his mind and he looked away, scorn briefly taking the place of fear in his thoughts.

Only then did he look at the King and Queen of Mercia, to whom he would have to answer for his invasion of their land.

'Let us begin,' King Aelfrid said.

'Begin,' said Queen Aethelwynne.

Handed a paper by one of the learned men of law, the King read out the terms of '*the Pope's surrender*'.

There was to be no negotiation. Almost all the demands to be made of the Pope through the person of the Abbot had been agreed in advance between the English and the Vikings. The Abbot was expected only to put his signature to the agreement.

Every soldier of the Redeemed was to be removed from English soil. Alonso was to take an oath that none of those who had invaded England would ever with his permission or to his knowledge set foot on it again. But he himself was to remain and face justice.

As he had led the Pope's Army, he was held to represent the Pope at these proceedings. As the Pope's representative, he was to agree to abandon all demands for taxes from the Christian kingdoms and earldoms of England. But there was to be no denial of advancement to English priests by way of penalizing the English people.

A lawyer brought pen and ink to Alonso, put the paper before him on the table, and pointed to the left side of it beneath the writing. He signed: 'Alonso de Llama, Nuncio'. It was not true that he was Nuncio. He had aspired to be Nuncio. And the King of Mercia had told him that here, now, he was the representative of the Pope. As such, was he not Nuncio? To sign the paper as Nuncio was a proud thing. It dignified him. It soothed away—for the moment—the humiliation of being a prisoner. He did not allow himself to think what was understood by all present, that if he refused to sign, he would certainly be executed, probably this very day, and by means the Vikings would perhaps decide.

The lawyer took the paper to the King, and pointed to the right side of it. 'Aelfrid Rex,' wrote the King of Mercia.

Commander Tostig put his mark—a rather well-drawn kitten—under the King's name, and the lawyer wrote 'Tostig Commander of the Viking Army' under the mark.

'Linkard.' wrote the Earl. And he guided the hand of Queen Bertha to write 'Bertha Regina'.

The lawyer wrote 'As witness' in the centre of the paper and passed it to Harald Goldmountain, who signed with a large M that stood out importantly on the page, with two dots above it.

Next was Mordec's turn.

When he saw Harald's signature he could not help exclaiming 'Aah!'.

The lawyer, taking the sound and the pause for the signs he expected that the Viking could not write, said, 'Just a mark will do.' But Mordec picked up the quill, and the lawyer watched with surprise as the words appeared fast and clear: 'Mordec son of Hauk'.

Father Donlock put a small Christian cross after his name.

Sir Baz wrote 'Sebastian Knight of the Empire', with a curlicue under each word.

'As there is no Emperor at present,' he commented mournfully, 'I as well as any other knight can stand for the laity of Christendom'.

Earl Reginald turned to Father Donlock when the signing was done. 'Is the agreement too unfair to the Church? I ask *you*, not the Abbot. We do not want to make a lasting enemy of Rome. Do we demand too much?'

'Considering that Abbot Alonso persuaded the Pope to this rude attempt to put us under his rule as though he had the right of a king in these islands, I don't believe our demands are excessive. I do not believe the Holy Father will think so either. His culprit is Abbot Alonso, not the people of England. And that is why I now urge that Alonso de Llama be sent to the Holy Father himself for justice to be done as the Vicar of Christ thinks best.'

'No, no!' Mordec cried out. 'Return him to the Pope? No! That would be to let him off. He is my prisoner. It is for me to decide his fate.'

On hearing this, Alonso clasped his crucifix tightly under the table, squeezed his eyes shut and moved his cherry-red lips in silent prayer.

'Commander?' Mordec said, expecting Tostig to support his demand.

The Commander both endorsed and amended Mordec's declaration.

'The prisoner is rightfully ours,' he declared.

'I could have a special cage built for him,' Harald Goldmountain offered.

'The right to pronounce this man's sentence belongs to me,' Mordec said firmly. 'Not only did he lead the army we defeated—'

'Helped to defeat,' King Aelfrid said.

'Helped,' his Queen said.

Mordec went on as if he had not heard the interruption.

'I captured him. And on top of all that, he was my personal enemy. He long sought to do me harm.'

'We are not now in the land where Viking law rules.' the King said mildly.

'Not now,' said the Queen.

The Earl spoke:

'I know, Mordec, that in Viking law, the injured person decides the punishment of the injurer. But we are talking now of the concerns of two nations, not of one man. Because we do not all live under the same laws, we came together here to reach decisions all could agree upon.'

'Perhaps if you tell us what you would do with the prisoner if he were put in your hands, we can judge whether it serves our purposes,' Queen Bertha said. 'Speaking for myself, I would feed him to my lioness, a service I would gladly render and I leave it open for your general approval.'

'It has *my* approval,' Sir Baz said, opening his eyes wide for once and looking quite cheerful.

Alonso shut his eyes and prayed again.

'I haven't decided,' Mordec confessed. 'Until I do, Commander Tostig will take charge of him, and the illustrious lord Harald Goldmountain will have him put in a cage.'

One of the lawyers shook his head strenuously to indicate his total disapproval. The other whispered in the King's ear, and the King nodded.

'Take him,' he said. 'But see to it that the terms of the agreement are enforced.'

* * *

A platoon of Vikings was waiting to put chains on the prisoner and ride him through the night to Barleyfield Monastery. Commander Tostig and Mordec rode with them. Harald Goldmountain was driven in a new chariot he had bought in Tamworth.

Earl Reginald, Father Donlock, and Queen Bertha went home.

King Aelfrid invited Sir Baz to sit with him awhile at the round table. They drank dark wine from crystal chalices. The doors stood open. Crickets sang in the courtyard. The candles burnt low in the candelabra on the walls. The guards kept discreetly out of sight.

'In a dream,' the King said, 'I sat here with twelve knights. There were no women or priests or villains or common folk with us. We talked about making the world a better place.'

'It can only get worse,' Sir Baz assured him.

harald goldmountain's greatest reward

There was no booty gained from this war; mere mementos were kept by the Vikings; weapons and armour, rings and brooches; a few gold or jewel-studded crucifixes.

But Harald Goldmountain had it in mind to reward the most deserving of the warriors.

He enjoyed being generous. He devised a plan for a grand ceremony to be held on his ship in the harbour of Barleyfield Monastery.

Harald had ten small model ships made, each about as long as his arm and as deep as the handle of a battleaxe. They had finely made sails with red and white vertical stripes. He himself filled each of them with gold and silver coins, counted out to the last coin on the Lombards' benches in Gaudia Brevis and brought to Harald by his own carts and ships over land and sea. They were to be bestowed upon the captains.

Next there were two larger models holding even more coins. One was for Daedalus, who had devised the catapults and the moveable walls of fire, those weapons of mass-killing which had greatly helped the Vikings to victory. The other was for someone as yet unnamed—'Just someone, you'll see who', Harald replied when asked for a name.

Last there was one model ship, the largest of all, heaped high with the glittering coins, that everyone knew, without Harald's saying, was for Commander Tostig.

The 'treasure ships' as Harald called them, were lined up on a long table stretching across his deck. His gold chair was placed behind it. The smaller ships were to his left, the larger ones to his right, and at the end of the line was a sealed barrel painted white.

When Harald himself carried it there he did not seem to be bearing anything heavy. It could not be full of gold and silver. Yet, everyone was sure, it must be something of great value.

Curiosity stoked the excitement among the crowd gathered to watch the ceremony from the quays. Harald's splendid ship was moored stern-on at the centre of the longest jetty, and hundreds of Vikings, servants, some visiting Mercian soldiers, and boys from Linkard in the green uniforms they proudly continued to wear, stood waiting expectantly, or sat on the wall or roof of the monastery.

Harald himself had not yet appeared. Bernie stood behind his chair, his crew along the sides of the ship, Leif among them.

Leif guessed that Mordec was one of those who name would be called out, and would come to receive an award, which in Mordec's case was (Leif knew without being told) whatever was in that barrel.

Leif kept looking at it. 'If I could lift it,' he thought, 'if I could feel its weight, I might be able to guess what's in it.'

His curiosity got the better of him. He edged towards the barrel. He looked about him. No one seemed to be taking any notice of him. He climbed on to the table, took the barrel in his hands, lifted it, and was surprised at its lightness.

'Leave that! Put it down!'

It was Harald's voice roaring at him.

Harald had just stepped out from his cabin on to the deck, in heavy robes of purple and white, to start the ceremony, when the first thing he saw was the orphan boy who always clung close Mordec, trying to steal the white barrel.

Leif started with fright, his hands shot up, throwing the barrel into the air and over the side of the ship into the water. He leapt off the table on to the deck and looked for a way to dodge the angry man descending upon him.

There was no escape. Harald seized him by the wrist and lifted him over the side. He held him there while he leant over and shouted, 'Go and find it in the sea, and don't come back until you ...'

The thin arm slipped out of his grip, and Leif splashed into the water.

A murmur sounded among those of the crowd who were near enough to see what had happened. All that remained in Harald's hand was a silver-chain bracelet.

He glanced at it in surprise—he'd hardly been aware of feeling it—and was about to throw it aside when a wide flat link in it caught his attention. He straightened up, he lifted the chain closer to his eyes, he read the name on the long link of solid silver.

'Leif,' he murmured. A recognition, a remembrance broke over him; of his wife showing him what she had had made for their little son. He heard her voice again, saying, 'The bracelet is too big for him now, but as soon as he's old enough to wear it, you will put it on his wrist.' And he remembered doing as she had wanted him to do, on the boy's second birthday, a few days before he was lost. He remembered something else too, turned the link over, and saw an M with gold dots over it—his signature.

'Leif! LEIF!'

In a moment he was over the side, dropping into the water with the bracelet still clutched in his hand, down, down deep into the water to find his lost son.

He soared up like a sea-monster, the water pouring from his head and shoulders, and looked about him desperately.

The crowd watched Leif swimming for the jetty, struggling to escape the man who was so angry with him that he had even jumped into the sea to come after him.

'LEIF! STOP! WAIT!'

But the boy swam on, his arms whipping the water, his feet churning up a foam in his hurry to get away from the wrath that was pursuing him.

Though his heavy ceremonial robes hampered him, Harald Goldmountain's passion to catch his son overcame all difficulty, sped him forward until he could reach the boy.

As his hand caught an arm, as his arms went round the slender body, the boy struggled, flung his limbs about, yelling 'No! No! Let me go!'

But Harald only held him tighter, until the boy gave up and stared up into the face of his captor, which was smiling, though wet with sea water and—could it be with tears? Water was pouring from the man's eyes!

Harald kissed the small wet head and looked into his eyes, green as his wife's had been. 'Be still! You are my son, my son!'

Leif stared at the smiling face in astonishment, and then, slowly, let his head fall on to the breast of the man. He was crying too, held in the strong arms of Harald Goldmountain. His father!

***

Only later Harald thought of asking Leif if he had always worn the bracelet.

'No. I lost it. I forgot about it. Then Mordec's father Hauk showed it to me and asked if I had ever had one like it. And I remembered it.'

'You really did remember it?'

'Yes I remembered mine had two humps on the back, and gold spots. I looked for them and they were there. I knew how to read then. I saw the two humps made the letter M. But I didn't know what it meant.'

'M for a Mountain,' Harald said, 'crowned with gold.'

And again he hugged his son. His son.

***

The ceremony that took place that day on Harald Goldmountain's big ship did not go quite as planned.

Leif's memory of it was forever after to remain blurred, as though the sea water was still in his eyes as he looked at everything going on about him.

He would remember standing on the table between the large and smaller model ships; many men cheering, raising flagons and beakers and drinking horns; his father, Harald Goldmountain, lifting him and embracing him over and over again, laughing his tremendous laugh that set the crowd laughing with him.

He would remember the hands of his father, Harald Goldmountain, fastening his bracelet back on his wrist. He would not remember how he came to be in dry clothes, only knew they must have been put on him by Bernie, who was to tend him often after that, the dark-skinned barefooted man with his big gold ear-rings and the cutlass in his sash.

And at some stage his father, Harald Goldmountain, was also in dry garments, all of embroidered gold, and was sitting on his golden chair with Leif standing between his knees.

'Leif, my son, you will make the awards.'

And one by one, as their names were called out by Bernie, the captains stepped on to the ship, heaved up the treasure-ship that Leif touched to show which was his, and carried it off to the applause of the multitude.

Then, 'Daedalus.' Bernie called.

Daedalus, who knew Leif well, ruffled the boy's hair before he and a fellow Viking (whom he had brought on board with him, having been forewarned of the weight of his reward) carried off his model ship with its glittering cargo.

Harald clapped his hands for silence and rose.

'Now, Leif my son, and all you warriors, I have a surprise for you. Please let that man pass.'

It was a surprise indeed. The crowd on the quay parted to let a man through who was wearing a red tunic with a white cross on it—and a helmet with a yellow plume.

A silence fell as the enemy soldier stepped on to the ship and made his way to face Harald Goldmountain across the table.

'Take off your helmet,' Harald commanded.

The man took it off and held it under his arm. The fair head of a young man was revealed, seen only from behind by the crowd.

'What have you done to earn the reward I am giving you?' Harald called out loudly.

'I have killed many Christian soldiers,' came the reply, in as loud a tone so all could hear, 'and saved many Viking lives'.

The crowd broke into a brief hubbub, silenced when Harald raised his right hand.

'Commander Tostig says you are the best fighter he has ever seen wielding a sword,' Harald said.

'I am proud of it,' came the reply.

'Now tell us your name.'

'My name,' said the man in the Christian tunic, 'is Horsa son of Harvald.'

He turned round then to face the crowd, and the Vikings from Trygghaven knew him instantly. They cheered and laughed and called out to him, and he shook a fist at them, smiling.

'The man I nearly killed!' Mordec remembered, with both horror and relief.

Harald's laugh rose above the rest, and Leif laughed with him, in happiness, until he lost his breath. Then Harald suddenly frowned.

'Weren't you afraid that a Viking would kill you?' he asked.

'I was more afraid that I might kill a Viking,' Horsa replied, which set Harald laughing again.

Three of Harald's men helped Horsa carry away his treasure. The applause did not stop until he had disappeared through the monastery gate.

A drum was sounded, then a trumpet. The crowd stood quiet and still. The name 'Commander Tostig' was called.

The Commander stepped on to the deck, stood and waved to the cheering crowd. When there was silence he made a speech, praising the soldiers who had 'fought as I expected Vikings to fight', he said. He unrolled a scroll and read out the names of the Vikings who had died in the battle, among them (the giant man) Svavar the Trader, and Hengist the Fisherman (father of Daedalus). 'We honour them as the gods are now honouring them in Valhalla.'

The crowd cheered, and called out 'Heroes! Heroes!'

The Commander turned to face Harald.

'Taking it upon myself to speak for every man in our army,' he said in ringing tones, 'I thank you, Harald

Goldmountain, illustrious lord, for seeing to it that every man had the best of weapons, stout armour, and all the food he needed to make him strong.'

And turning again to the crowd, he announced that, thanks to Harald Goldmountain, every fighter would receive five gold coins—which roused long applause.

At last Leif could touch the Commander's model ship before four men came and carried it away for the Commander.

Harold turned to Bernie.

'That is the end of the ceremony,' he said. 'You can tell them it's over, send them away.'

'But … Mordec!' Leif said.

'Mordec? Oh yes, I had forgotten Mordec.'

'His award is in the sea. I dropped it there.'

'Mordec's award? It doesn't matter now. It was only a paper.'

'What did the paper say?'

'It said that I was making over all my Northumbrian estates to him. But now I've found you, my son, my real son, those lands must be yours when you grow up.'

'Then can I give them to Mordec?'

'You can do anything you like with them when they are yours.'

'So is Mordec getting no reward today? Wasn't he the one the leader of the Christians surrendered to?'

'You want Mordec to have a reward? Does Mordec matter very much to you?' Harald asked, feeling a small pang of jealousy.

'Yes, because I own him. He was magicked to me. And I kept him alive when we were lost.'

'Master,' Bernie murmured in Harald's ear. 'The people expect Mordec's name to be called.'

'Shall we call him, Leif?'

Leif nodded.

So Mordec's name was called, and the crowd cheered loud and long as he came on to the ship in his dark blue tunic.

He was the first to speak as he came up to the table. Bending forward and peering over his glasses which he moved to the end of his nose, he said quietly:

'Harald, I want you to know that I guessed some time ago that Leif was your son. But I thought it best if you found it out for yourself. If you hadn't found out by now, I planned to tell you today. The final proof was your signature on the surrender agreement—the same M with the dots as on the back of the bracelet. You have him now. He has you. He'll be your right-hand man. You won't need me any more.'

He began to turn away, pushing his glasses back in place, but Leif called out, 'Mordec. Don't go!'

'Set me free, Leif,' Mordec said, laughing. 'That can be my reward.'

'He had a paper all ready in the barrel that I dropped in the sea. It would have made you a sort of king.'

'Let it rest there. Now he has you and you have him, please, my owner, let me go.'

But Leif did not look happy.

'I planned something else for your reward, Mordec,' Harald said. 'As the last thing in the ceremony, I was in fact intending to bestow a title on you.'

'A title? What title?'

'The title of "Mordec the Conqueror".'

'That is a great honour,' Mordec said seriously. 'I could ask for nothing better. I accept the honour. I believe it is rightfully mine. Alonso tried to hunt me down. But I made him beg me on his knees to spare him. I made him give up his sword to me. I want to keep that sword.'

Harald nodded slowly. He thought, but did not say, that Abbot Alonso had been brought to his knees by two whole armies, not just the anger of one Viking. But he could see anger now igniting in Mordec's eyes behind their glasses at the mere thought of the Abbot, and decided to say no more about it. Whether Commander Tostig and King Aelfrid would allow Mordec to keep the sword, time would tell.

'Will you feast with us tonight to celebrate the reunion of my son and me? We will piece together, Leif and you and I, the story of how he was lost, and found by you, and brought home so he and I could find each other again.'

'I will.'

'Bernie, I will announce that *Mordec the Conqueror* is leaving the ship. So let the trumpet sound again, and the drum. Let the crowd cheer as they have never cheered before. Leif and I will lead the cheering.'

'Yes, yes!' Leif shouted. 'Mordec the Conqueror!'

And delighting in his boy, Harald Goldmountain again laughed his tremendous laugh.

the brides' song

The victorious, invincible, Viking army sailed home to the Northlands on a night when the gods showed their pleasure by draping the whole sky with curtains of crimson and purple and green, their hems falling to the smooth surface of the water. They rippled, they billowed, they swirled out to the rim of the world. Each burst of rich colour started high above the ships, descended round them and upon them. The sea took on the colours, so it seemed the ships flew, not under the sky and on the sea, but through the sky.

Old men, children, and many young women wait on the cliffs and quays to watch the sails flocking towards them through the glory.

On the outermost point of the pier wall stands Delfinola, dressed in a crimson robe and the rings and brooches of a king. The dawn wind that fills the sails of the ships, streams out her white hair. The leading ship—the fastest—is Captain Bjarwulf's, and she knows before she sees that her beloved husband Pelf is standing in the prow, looking for her as keenly as she is for him. Beside her, Thorgerd the Daft will wave when she waves—but will give a shout of joy all her own when she sees Mordec come safely home.

And there he comes, the conquering hero!

Close behind Bjarwulf's ship sail two side by side, Commander Tostig's and Harald Goldmountain's.

Harald sits in his gold chair, watching the sky.

On either side of him stand Mordec and Leif, and behind him Bernie. All are silent with awe, entranced. Then Harald laughs a laugh of triumph so enormous it surely reaches the ears of the gods, sways the heavens' curtains of light, and is the first sound from the fleet that the watchers on the harbour hear.

And look there! See all the ships of the huge fleet, sail upon sail upon sail, spread over the visible ocean, bringing home a generation of young men who have fought their first war and won.

When they land, the blare of trumpets will sound through the cheers, and pipes and drums will beat and trill, and young women waiting with garlands of flowers have a new song to sing to them, which Delfinola composed.

Whether it will be sung, and if so whether it will be heard through the clamour of greeting, they will soon know.

These are the words of it:

The Brides' Song

Let loose your hair my daughter fair
And clothe yourself in purest white,
He's coming on a milk-white mare.
I'll crown your head with candlelight,
I'll call him in, your chosen groom,
I'll spread a feast before you twain,
And happiness will fill the room,
And you will laugh and dance again.
Then slow the stars will turn above
And slow the winter will go past,
But sure you'll hold your cherished love
Till May bring back the spring at last.
You'll rock the cradle, bake the bread,
And see your sons grow tall and strong,
And crown in turn your daughter's head,
And live in peace where you belong.

what else happened

When Mordec's mother Estrid heard that Harald Goldmountain had found his son—no other than Leif, the boy whom Mordec had brought home with him and she had fondly mothered—she went to the chest where she kept the letter Harald Goldmountain had written to her to say that he would make Mordec his heir if he never found his son, took it to the hearth and threw it on the fire.

Only after that did she tell Mordec and Hauk about it.

'It's a good thing you didn't tell me before I took Leif with me to the war,' Mordec said in a mock gruff voice, 'or who knows what dire fate he might have come to so that I could inherit Harald's empire!'

Then Mordec took up the sword that Abbot Alonso had surrendered to him, held it across his palms, and said, 'This is worth more to me than a mountain of gold. When it was laid on my hands by the conquered enemy, *I stood for all the Vikings.*'

And Hauk, Estrid and Eyrin could not have been more proud of him.

* * *

Gus and Lily married of course. Father Donlock performed the ceremony in the church of Linkard

Castle, with Rorick acting as the father of the bride just before he started on the long journey back to Queen Gloria in Italy laden with captured weapons and other unsuitable gifts from the daughter to the mother.

He had come with other Vikings in good standing from Italy. Goldmountain ships had carried them to England from Genova.

He had brought the gift of a large diamond to Queen Bertha. After the battle it helped him to make his peace with her. She was, he found, as beautiful as he remembered her.

* * *

Some time later, Mordec wrote to Lily—sending the letter through Mel de Gustybuss—to ask her to be his envoy in a delicate matter that needed to be settled.

She replied that she would very much like to do it; that she and Gus—as Mordec had expected—would go on the journey together. Mel told them that they needed royal robes for this affair. To his surprise (for he had known Lily all her life, and knew well what she liked to wear) she agreed.

So it was that they travelled royally attired to the Welsh country of Owaindale. They sailed in a borrowed Goldmountain ship to the Welsh port of Sveinsey, then rode in a carriage with polished horses, the crew riding beside them as their guards and attendants, to Owaindale.

Queen Bertha had sent messengers a month ahead requesting Princess Angharad to grant her daughter an audience, and the Princess, without asking why because she guessed the answer, had agreed. She received the young Queen and her consort with all due ceremony.

It was sad news that Queen Lily had come in person to break to the Princess, the assembled courtiers, and through them to the nation.

Maredudd the short dark mine owner and his tall fair daughter Tegwen, who had once been betrothed to Prince Madoc, stood in the forefront of the gathering as Queen Lily said what she'd come to say.

And Fletch the huntsman, who had gone with a contingent of soldiers from Owaindale to England at the behest of the late lamented King of Cornwall to augment the forces of the English in the face of invasion; and had been saved from an annihilating ambush by none other than the Prince of Owaindale himself; and who now, as a result of that venture, bore the title of Commander, stood near the throne in a scarlet uniform with the princedom's highest award, the Medal of Honour, hanging on his chest.

('So this was Mordec's princedom,' Gus was to say to Lily when later they were alone together. 'Why did he ever return to Trygghaven?' 'Because here he would have come to nothing,' Lily told him. 'I've always understood Mordec better than you.')

A wail went up and many wept when Queen Lily regretfully announced that Prince Madoc had died in the war.

The Princess silently clasped the Queen's hand.

Tegwen fainted and was caught by her husband Cledwyn.

Fletch stood stiff as a poker blinking tears away.

Princess Angharad dropped the hand of the Queen to cover her face with both her own. But she took them away and clasped them together as the Queen's consort, the Lord Gus, went on to say that he, Prince Madoc, had fought valiantly on the side of the English, and had fallen only after slaying ten enemy soldiers. He could not be brought back for burial, because the Vikings had mistaken him for one of their own, and had sent him in a burning ship to Valhalla before King Aelfrid's men had been able to find him among the dead. But both the Vikings and the English swore that he would never be forgotten; that he was a hero in the annals of both nations, to be held in high honour forever.

The Princess declared a month of mourning, and said how proud she was of her brother, and how proud she knew his people were, who had always loved him dearly.

When the folk gathered outside the palace heard the sad yet inspiring news of their Prince's heroic death, they sang the song they had sung every evening looking towards the hill that had captured him, until he had come back to them:

Prince of our hearts
Come home to us
We long for you so!

Though the words begged him to come back to them, the slow, sad, painfully beautiful rendering of the song acknowledged that he would never return, that this time he was gone forever.

When the Queen, the Lord Gus, the Princess, and Cadfan the Chancellor were alone behind closed doors, sitting comfortably with mulled wine and hot soup to warm them, the Princess said, 'That was tragic news indeed. I thank you for coming this long way to break it to me. We will erect a statue of our Prince on the hill where once he disappeared for ten years. His memory will be kept alive for as long as there is a land called Owaindale. Now, dear friends, tell me. Do you have news of Mordec son of Hauk? Is he well?'

* * *

Sir Baz found himself the unexpected heir to the property of Sir Cedric—a villa and all it contained, including a large stock of excellent wines, presided over by a taciturn Scottish servant who might or might not have been deaf, and whom Sir Baz retained.

The aging English knight had died of natural causes shortly before the invasion of England by the Army of the Redeemed, so was unable to fulfil a clause in his contract with the Earl to command the Linkard Guards in time of war.

In his will, Sir Cedric explained that he owed his life to Sir Baz who had spared it when they had jousted a few years earlier; and he also declared that he could imagine no better successor to him in the job of Knight Champion of the Earldom of Linkard than Sir Baz.

The Earl offered Sir Baz the job, and the knight accepted it, on the understanding that he would remain Knight Champion to Queen Bertha.

'So there must never be enmity between the Earldom of Linkard and the Fenreach,' Sir Baz cautioned.

Both the Earl and the Queen solemnly agreed to commit themselves to life-long friendship with each other.

Sir Baz asked that the bondsmen be set free as a reward for fighting gallantly under his command in the service of the Earl. 'They also trailed the Abbot and helped to capture him,' he said.

The Earl agreed.

Lady Jessica said, 'As we no longer, thank heaven, have Mistress Pillikin and Master Hitchem to guard and supervise them, they are in fact already free, and from now on will stay that way.'

***

Harald Goldmountain spent more time in a castle he built on his Northumbrian estates than in any of his other grand homes.

Soon after the war, he took his son, Leif, on a voyage back to the Welsh country where the boy had spent most of his early years.

Viking though he was, all the people of Runnydale received Harald with courtesy, mixed with awe when Zarath of the East told them how extremely rich he was.

Slate embraced Leif, and asked him for the whole story of what had happened to him and Mordec after he'd set them on the path to freedom. Leif told it dramatically, exaggerating both the hardship they had endured and the grandeur they had enjoyed. Then, remembering this was Wales, he begged Slate to keep the secret of Mordec not really being the prince of Owaindale. Fortunately, Slate was used to keeping secrets, and he kept this one too.

Harald asked the rulers, separately, what each of them would most like him to give their nation as a reward for 'caring for and schooling my son'.

Strangely enough—or it would be strange if Slate had not had something to do with it—they both, for once, gave the same answer. They would like a harbour where trading ships could offload and take on cargo. Harold had it built for them, Runnydale became a regular trading port, and the people prospered.

The Princess Starling persuaded Zarath of the East to marry her. She had become slim and good-looking by following the magic rituals he prescribed for her.

Zarath continued to grant wishes by magic on one night in the year, and the story of how he had once magicked a Viking boy into existence to be a friend to Leif son of Harald Goldmountain became part of the folklore of the small country.

* * *

Crispin Cuthburd, the poet and diplomat, never did complete his epic about the war. But he did propose marriage to Lady Jessica, who courteously refused him (to the secret relief of Queen Aethelwynne, who had never met her but knew by intuition that she was not a suitable match for a man as sensitive as Crispin).

A year after the war, Jessica married George, the nephew and heir of the tragic King Mark of Cornwall, and thus became queen of that country.

When Jessica told George that she had good friends among the Vikings, she and George sent two messengers to Trygghaven to ask for help in finding out how King Mark had died.

Gunnar and Titch led the Cornishmen to Lovehaven.

Bjarwulf greeted them amiably, listened to their question, and replied that the King had fought bravely for his life with him, Bjarwulf.

When the fatal blow was struck, 'by me', the King had 'fallen back into the arms of an old man named Bruce, who took the sword from his hand and fought on until he too was pierced with a mortal thrust', again administered by Bjarwulf himself.

Bjarwulf said he remembered it all very clearly, and thought at the time how skilfully the King wielded his weapon.

'But he was no match for me,' Bjarwulf said. 'He should not have challenged me. I fought rough and dirty. I never lost a fight in all my working years.'

He sent his wishes for a happy life and many children to the young King of Cornwall and his English queen.

'And an apology?' one of the messengers suggested.

Bjarwulf looked puzzled.

'What for?' he asked.

King George and Queen Jessica lived for most of the year in their island castle. To that destination,

Earl Reginald and the ruling family of the Fenreach with Sir Baz, and Harald Goldmountain with his son Leif, and now and then with Leif's friend Eyrin brother of Mordec, sailed in Harald's ship when the seas were calm and the breeze was steady and warm, all being frequent summer guests.

The eldest son of King George and Queen Jessica, who would in time become King Mark II of Cornwall, would also eventually inherit the Earldom of Linkard.

* * *

King Aelfrid bestowed the title of Countess of Felldown on Dellibeth, heir to the lands and castle of the extinct Cogg family.

Countess Dellibeth invited the dancer who had saved her property from the Army of the Redeemed to make her home at Cogg Hall. But Charlotte could not stay in one place.

With the active help of Mel de Gustybuss, her agent and chief costume designer and artistic director, she became famous in all the great houses of Europe, and even in Asia and Egypt, for the grand and curious spectacles of dance with which she entertained the monarchs, the pashas, the caliphs, the archbishops, and even the Popes. Successive Popes.

For the old Pope died, and was succeeded by a younger man, who before long was succeeded by another old man; and Charlotte was to meet many a Pope, and many a prince who would have made her his wife had she been willing, before she retired from her career and did settle down at last, laden with a treasury of gifts beyond price, at Felldown.

'East, West, England is best' was her verdict—which future Earls, descended from Dellibeth's brother, adopted as the motto of the Felldown arms.

* * *

And what became of Abbot Alonso?

Tostig and Mordec had had a lively discussion on their ride from Tamworth to Barleyfield after the Round Table conference, as to whether he should have his limbs hacked off and his trunk opened up, his rib cage spread like angel wings, his trunk stuck on a pole, and the grisly monument to the invaders' defeat planted in the burnt grass where the ashes of thousands of his Christian soldiers lay on the field above Barleyfield Ridge—or not.

They discussed the matter loudly, staying close to the chained prisoner.

Alonso sagged and drooped in his saddle, silent, even his red lips pale, his eyes squeezed shut in terror.

Tostig said he could simply be kept in a deep dark damp dungeon.

Mordec said that was not a bad idea, but as the wretch was really his prisoner, he had given the matter some thought, and on the whole he couldn't think of anything the Abbot would hate more—short of torture, upon hearing which word the prisoner had uttered an involuntary groan—than to have to obey the orders of someone else.

What Mordec had in mind he said—and what eventually was done—was this: Alonso was taken to

Holy Island in the far north-east of Northumbria, where there was the largest monastery in all the Western Isles, called Lindisfarne.

Nearly two hundred years before our story began, Lindisfarne had been sacked by Vikings, and though it was restored, the monks never knew when the same might happen again.

There, on the 'suggestion' of Commander Tostig, Alonso would lead the life of a simple working monk.

If ever he gave the least trouble—Mordec told him in as many words—the notion of those bony angel wings and that tall pole would be revived.

So Alonso was taken to Lindisfarne, and there he stayed for the remaining few years of his life.

* * *

At Mordec's insistence, as part of the terms of surrender by Abbot Alonso (representing the Church of Rome), his Abbey and the half of the island on which it stood, was ceded to Sam of the West who already owned the other half.

Sam turned the entire edifice into a centre for the study of nature and astronomy. In time, historians came to refer to it as 'the first university', though the claim was much disputed in later centuries by theologians and doctors in the universities of Bologna, Paris, and Oxford.

Daedalus went to work there. He revealed to Sam who it was had kept him informed of Alonso's plans.

'Horsa posed as a Christian convert and was appointed bodyguard to the Abbot. I was the only one who knew, but he'd made me swear to keep his secret until the war was over.'

Daedalus had designed and helped to build the devices that shot many rocks at a time, and the fiery walls on wheels which had come together like a pair of jaws to consume a great part of Alonso's army.

His father, Hengist the Fisherman, having perished on the battlefield, Daedalus sent him to Valhalla in his own burning ship one fine morning.

And beside him he laid Svein the Carter who had also fallen in the war and had no son to perform his funeral rites. As Svein was his father's friend, Daedalus would not let him be borne with most of the Viking dead to be buried in a mound in Northumbria. He set the two warriors drifting into the dawn to be welcomed together in Odin's hall.

***

Among the novelties Daedalus designed at Sam's academy were an engine moved by steam, a winged chair that could fly on currents of air, and—in collaboration with Eyrin son of Hauk—a machine that could add, subtract, multiply and divide numbers.

The Church declared it to be a 'Satanic device' and threatened all those who would use it with painful consequences, so it was discarded and its secret is lost.

The academy on the island is now a museum where you can see the original designs and prototypes of many other inventions by Sam's students and their masters, but not the calculating machine which awaits reinvention.

* * *

Horsa became a sub-commander of the Viking army under Tostig. In time he succeeded the great Commander and became as great in reputation. His red tunic with the white cross and his helmet with the yellow plume were displayed in his tent in all his campaign.

* * *

The Treaty of Tamworth kept peace between the English and the Vikings for many years.

The Vikings gave up their village on the Nijn river, and returned Barleyfield Monastery to its abbot, but held Northumbria under their own law, farming the land and establishing towns and cities.

They became as English as King Aelfrid had wished. They ceased to make raids into other parts of the island, and apart form some skirmishes with the Scots, lived peacefully enough for their agriculture and commerce to flourish.

* * *

Julius the Troll lived to a great age—he was nearly 200 years old when he died, if the Skalds are to be believed—and bequeathed his underground palace and all his possessions to his assistant Roxane and the dwarves.

The news of his death spread among his correspondents in an unusual way. Sam of the West, Zarath of the East, Adam the Lombard, Mel de Gustybuss and many others found pigeons on their window sills with no messages tied to their legs. Thus it could be said that they brought home the silence that was the Troll's last message.

What happened to the subterranean palace and its riches after Roxane and the dwarves died, no one knows. But after all these years, travellers still report that sounds of music rise mysteriously through the snow in that region, causing their dogs to prick up their ears and howl.

* * *

And what—most necessary to be told—became of the hero of our story, Mordec, and his family?

His father Hauk went back to tending his orchard, honeybees, and meadmaking.

From time to time the Skald, and other lesser skalds, came to the mead hall to sing their songs and repeat their sagas—among which the Saga of Mordec was a favourite.

Eyrin spent many a summer with Leif and Bernie in the great house of Harald Goldmountain in Northumbria, or on the island of the King and Queen of Cornwall. When he grew up, he chose to go to Sam's academy to study mathematics. He became, as all the history books of the period record, the most famous mathematician of his time, contributing a body of work that has inspired generations of mathematicians down to our own day. The 'Eyrin Conjecture' is still a wonder and a delight to young mathematicians.

But you were asking—what of Mordec himself?

261

Mordec did not stay long in Trygghaven. He went to study law and nature for a while at Sam's academy as he had long wanted to do. But Harald Goldmountain found he could not do without him; not only because Leif often spoke of him and plainly missed him, but also because Harald himself wanted his company. So Mordec returned to England and became the overseer of Harald's 'empire', as Mordec called it.

What he achieved for Harald and himself was the merging of two great commercial establishments: the House of Goldmountain and the House of Adam the Lombard, Mordec's grandfather.

Few historians have recorded that Vikings and Lombards worked together in harmony, but they did. No great venture could be paid for without the approval and assistance of Goldmountain & Adam. Its main offices were in the Lombard town of Gaudium Brevis in Italy—managed after Adam's death by his key-keeper, Clavi—and the Goldmountain palace in Northumbria; and its busiest branch was in London.

Mordec moved between them as the man who had the power of decision; whether to invest money in a project or not. Mordec decreed that a castle may or may not be built here, a cathedral there, a bridge, a harbour, a city; and his 'yes' or 'no' allowed or disallowed many a war and invasion.

Discreetly, almost unnoticeably, Mordec the Conqueror dominated the age.

When Bjarwulf the Pirate retired from his dangerous career—letting Lars take his place as master of the Serpent King—his accountant Pelf went to work for Goldmountain and Adam in London, and found out at last what the lists of numbers and names that Captain Anwid had been carrying on The Good Ship Good were all about.

His wife, Delfinola, enjoyed life in the city more than she had expected to, and became an acclaimed singer and song-writer. One of her most popular songs was 'The Lament of Captain Cogg', about a woman sea-captain who had sailed the seas on The Good Ship Good with a crew of warrior girls, had fought pirates, had lost her ship, and had finally died on an English shore defending her country from invaders.

Sadly, the song is lost, and so forever was The Good Ship Good.

Ten years after the war in England, Mordec married Harald Goldmountain's niece Adelaide, the beautiful daughter of the Duke of Normandy. By her choice, their house was built on the southern bank of the River Seine, where it still stands and is still lived in by their descendants.

Some of their descendants became Kings of France and Queens of England. None bore any noticeable resemblance to their Viking-Lombardian ancestor, except that a few of them were shortsighted.

***

A tapestry depicting the events of that era, including the story of Mordec, hangs on a wall of the Gaudin museum in Rouen. Started by the Countess Djil Gaudin, it was finished by many other hands, and is widely regarded as a reliable historical record up to the death of King Arthur of the Round Table.

There too is a small ship, modeled on a Viking longship, about half the usual size. The name painted on its bows is Foal of the Foam. But a note beside it informs the visitor that it is only a replica of the lost ship that Olaf the Shipbuilder built for Harald Goldmountain's son Leif, and which was abandoned and forgotten until found by Mordec son of Hauk when he was fourteen. He and his friends sailed in it, the note says, along with the Viking fleet, to raid England.

It was the voyage that carried him into these adventures.